Afraid of Me

Arthur West

PublishAmerica
Baltimore

Hardcover 978-1-4489-3084-5
Softcover 978-1-4489-4302-9
PUBLISHED BY PUBLISHAMERICA, LLLP
www.publishamerica.com
Baltimore

Printed in the United States of America

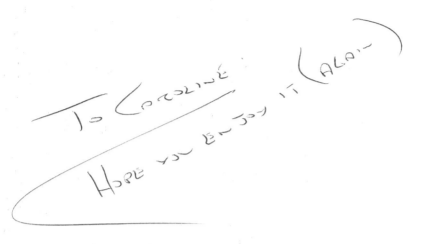

To those who have been patient with me.

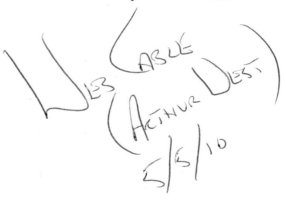

ONE

BAXTER COLLEGE
A While Ago

CHAPTER ONE

...And She Was Screaming

She wasn't particularly tall, nor was she very thin or extra heavy. She wasn't stunning or striking in any particular way. She was a pretty average girl at first glance. An average turn of hip into waist, out again to breast and slender shoulder, the kind that didn't call up real passion until seen curled up next to you. Amy Marie Hudson was *almost* plain. At five foot four and 115 pounds, with brown hair, brown eyes, she wore round, gold-framed, what you might think of as hippie-style eyeglasses. She had a few freckles sprinkled across her slightly pug nose and a little squint in her eye.

Amy looked at you with a slightly quizzical expression, almost as if she were trying to figure you out, or measure you up. Polite but never apologetic, that squint could put people immediately on guard, and almost as often as not, it did.

The overall package was not displeasing to the eye, but, especially with that unnerving look, did not often invite closer examination.

That is, unless you took the time to talk to her. Then you noticed her mouth. Her mouth was expressive, friendly, and open—not just hanging there open—but open as in inviting. A ready smile and a 'hello' always offered, her mouth was the only really sexy part about her. The rest you'd hardly notice. Most people didn't notice, back then anyway.

Back then was September of freshman year—Orientation Day at Baxter College in the Catskills. Old Baxter hosted its 113th opening that September and as had been done for a number of years before, this day welcomed the new class at the College by way of the College Camp Experience.

You see, the College owned what had once been a small retreat for clerics from the city. It was a couple of fields on the top of a peaceful little mountain, a pond and a big, rambling old house, complete with native stone fireplace and a big Great Room which was ideal for prayer, discussion or meeting.

Baxter had cut a couple of downhill trails along one side of the evergreen, maple, and birch covered mountain, had installed a clanking T-bar up the side of the biggest trail and cleared a cross-country trail over the other side of the mountain, across the high meadows to the campus three miles away. They had added a bunch of picnic tables under the pines, a couple of volleyball nets in the open fields around the big house and installed a caretaker of sorts in a cottage at the edge of the woods behind the pond.

This day the air around College Camp, as it was so creatively called, was filled with the voices of 400 newly arrived freshmen. Given a good, clean, fun introduction to college life, shown a good time before the upperclassmen could introduce them to the downtown bars, the College hoped a dose of mandatory fun in the form of volleyball, Frisbee, kites, nature walks and, of course hot dogs, soda, potato salad and chips, would get everyone off to the right start.

This, and after a good snow, were the only times the old camp was really busy. Sure, different groups, students or faculty, used the big house from time to time for overnight socials or meetings (read party) and the President's strategy retreats for his Leadership Team there always produced the budget compromises needed. But it never seemed quite as festive; it never quite competed with happy hour downtown, as well as when invaded by that group of bright-eyed and eager new students each September. The energy of that group gave the old place a vibrancy that it never otherwise had and for that matter, was probably never intended to have by the solitary priests who communed with hills and trees and quiet beauty before Baxter rescued it from a recession motivated oblivion.

And today the new students had energy to spare. Charged up with hot dogs and fresh air, the 400 new kids on the block had attacked the mountain. There were lots of sports—organized and otherwise. There was lots of walking and talking and getting to know you. And there was lots of nervousness about the campus over the hills and the semester to come.

Many of those new students feared the challenge of college. Many wondered if they would be up to the test. Some hid their fear with false bravado. Some hid it with a veneer of attitude. Still others didn't hide their fear at all but just used this day on the hill to consider what they were now up against.

Perhaps the luckiest were those who had not yet even considered what they were up against. Those, at least, were able to enjoy the day without reservations.

Amy Hudson feared it all, and more than just a little. But she looked at it from a somewhat unique perspective. Amy dealt with her fear in a different way than any of the other 400 odd students there that day. As Amy wandered the fields and watched the volleyball and breathed in the smells and freshness of her new experience, saying hello and smiling but not really joining in, a shy smile combined with a little aloofness, she was declaring the new start she had longed for.

Now that the day was fading, the sun beginning to sink behind the out-stretched arms of the pines, the new students had finally found something they could almost all get together on. Across the corner of the fire pond, they stretched a rope provided by the orientation staff and the tugs-of-war commenced. Once, twice and again the 400 split up into two sides and pulled and pulled until one side or the other was pulled into the water and drenched. As the Caretaker/Orientation Coordinator watched from his porch and the food service staff packed up the day's worth of debris, good clean fun was literalized by this impromptu baptism of the freshman class.

Already the leaders in the class were emerging. Those who were loudest, with the least fear it seemed, grabbed the rope near the water, took the lead and dared the other side to drag them into the water. It didn't really matter much which side a person was on. Both banks of the pond rose up from the water at about the same pitch and both dropped off sharply after the peak of the artificially made banks.

Since the setting for their baptism had originally been a fire pond—designed more to protect the big house than for its beauty—it had a dug-out center area and dikes on three sides to keep the water from the spring that was its source penned in. The water was cold to be sure but Baxter's newest didn't seem to mind. Caught up, as they were in the game, they saw only each other; felt only their excitement, fears and joys. They became, as the school had hoped and expected a community of students.

Amy Marie Hudson didn't grab the rope near the water. She feared the crowd and the brute force of the game. She tucked her straight brown hair behind her ear, looked over the top of those round-framed glasses and joined in though, for this was to be a new beginning for her. This was to be different from high school. This was to be her chance to try new things, to risk.

It had taken a lot of thought, this decision to risk new things. A lot of analyzing and deep consideration had been endured in the dark of the night. Amy Marie, as her Mom referred to her, had had a lot of time for that kind of thought in her high school years. Not exactly popular, too plain to attract a lot of attention from the boys and too shy to seek attention with her personality, she had spent most of her time in the library and with a small circle of people she called friends.

Her friends were her safe-zone. With them she was able to relax. While fear plagued most of her interactions with others, with these fellow outcasts she felt less fear. Rick and Sean and Maureen and Amy had been a team. Too big or too shy or too bookish, they had all struggled along at the edge of the mainstream of their peer group. They all had each other and all wanted more. They hung out, played guitars, sang and dreamed of being more than the quiet little group of weirdos on the edge of the larger school community.

Perhaps because of her lack of social opportunity, Amy had spent much of her high school years in the library. Her grades had been excellent and she had coasted into Baxter. A reasonably happy seeming little bookworm, she was in reality a self-defined social outcast looking to start over. Amy was determined that her college experience would be different. While others had gone to the prom, she had sat home and thought. She sat and she promised herself some things. And now was the time to begin to collect on those promises.

Amy Hudson joined in. She grabbed the rope and pulled. She attacked what she feared. She became a part of what she feared, and now she was screaming.

CHAPTER TWO

...It All Seemed So Simple

William Alexander Clark had approached his introduction to Baxter College in a different manner entirely, and for him, life had heretofore supplied few unknowns and fears. Although success in his schoolwork had not always come easily, he managed grades good enough to get into Baxter by applying himself. That had been his goal. Alex's life had been a series of goals which, each in their turn had been set and reached.

He had decided to go to college while in junior high school and to go to Baxter specifically, half way through high school. He had chosen Baxter because it was far enough away from home to enable him to stay away as it suited him but not too far that he couldn't conveniently get home when that suited him. It was a logical choice.

Baxter was cheap enough to afford but good enough to lead to medical school if he worked hard. It was big enough to avoid sticking out yet small enough to make a mark if and when he chose. And besides, his cousin Ted, who had attended Baxter six years earlier, had given the place a good report as far as girls and bars were concerned.

All these factors were considered as Alex chose. They were all requirements for the school that would fit into the plan he was creating for himself. Alex's life was to be a reasoned, managed one. His life was planned so as to provide shelter and to avoid fear. If comfort, security, and certainty could be attained, he reasoned, then the uncertainty that his parents told of—over and over and over again it seemed—of lives defined by the Great Depression and a World War, would not threaten. Careful planning would keep his life on track.

Both of Alex's parents' lives had been framed by the depression and the war. Dad, as a pre-teen, had watched his parents grow bitter and unhappy after his father had lost his Wall Street position in the crash of '29. Alex's grandmother, a prim and stern-faced tiny woman, had never allowed her husband to forget that she had had to go to work when the only work he could find was clerking in a hardware store.

Alex's Mom had collected scrap for the war effort as a teenager and pumped gas at the General Store when her brothers were called off to war. Her own widowed Mother's struggle with four children to feed and no work but other folks' laundry to do had caused Alex's Mom to grow conservative and cautious even as a young woman.

Dad's own war experience had made him long for nothing more than the security of a nine-to-five job and the little white Cape in Westchester that had been home to Alex until today. Conservatively built and gradually added on to as Alex and his siblings had arrived, the little house was the Clark's first home and their only home.

The two of them had drilled this need for security and certainty into Alex and the result was his own orderly approach to life.

Alex had reasoned in high school that to be popular one had to play a sport. At six foot four, basketball had been a natural choice for him. He chose of course to play, set himself the goal of making the team and ended up helping his high school to the regional title in his senior year.

Now came college. Now he set his sights on Baxter. The plan was to concentrate on the grades so that medical school could be a part of the future. All was to go according to plan.

There was a lingering guilt that Alex did not entirely understand regarding the abrupt way he had dismissed his Mom and Dad when they dropped him off on the first day of Orientation. It had made sense to him to jump right in and start controlling his own life, but the hurt look in his Mother's eye when he kept her from helping to unpack his Dad's old duffel bag and settle in wasn't part of the plan.

He had sent them off with a, "Well, I guess you'll both be wanting to get right back on the road." Alex's eyes were already checking out what his floor mates were carrying in. He had shifted his weight from foot to foot in impatience, wanting to explore, to visit up and down the hall, to compare his approach to everyone else's.

Dad had mumbled agreement, uncomfortable around so many young people, but Mom's eyes betrayed the anguish she would never outwardly speak. She felt that her eldest, her once shy little boy, was dismissing her. Dismissing her it seemed, from his life.

She reached up to hug his tall frame, reached her small arms around his big boned shoulders, ruffled his neatly combed sandy hair and squeezed him just a moment longer than she had intended to. She tried to tide herself over, build up a reserve of remembrance of her little boy to take back home with her. She looked over at his Dad, solid and rumpled and fidgeting to get out the door without a large show of emotion.

They shared the same broad, friendly face and wide-set eyes. She could see that Alex's nose was beginning to go in the slightly hooked direction that characterized the Clarks as they aged. Both had beards rough to the touch and both sets of ears were a little large. But Alex's full lipped mouth and sensitive green eyes she knew were hers.

14

She looked from one to the other, packed up the thoughts of the younger version in her mind to bring out as she lived on with the older version and sighed. She told her son that there would be homemade cookies in the mail soon and walked slowly back to the car with her older version.

The guilt Alex felt as they left confused him. There was no real reason for it he thought. He was sure that they understood. But he kept thinking about the trip home, and the silence that must have blanketed the car on the way back to Westchester.

The guilt worried him and he wondered why it should be one of his first new experiences at college. After all, didn't he have it all planned out?

Alex immediately noticed the girls at college and this experience he felt more to his liking. This was one of the rewards of careful planning, he thought. In high school, along with the popularity that a varsity letter brought, as planned, had also come the attention of some of the girls that Alex longed to get to know. Painfully shy as a child, he sought for a way out of his shyness and found it in lay ups and foul shots. Encouraged by the cheers of the loyal high school fans, his shyness dropped away and he learned what he thought of as a pretty cool approach with the opposite sex. Several of the nicest and several of the less nice but more cooperative girls had become his company for a while. And it was then that he had noticed a difference in the girls he was attracted to.

College girls (women) now proved the flavor of Alex's taste. It was not the flashy Daddy's girls from Long Island or the "rich bitches" from Connecticut, as his new roommate referred to them, to whom he was drawn. Alex found himself attracted to, and would find success of sorts with, the plainer but pretty girls who were overlooked at first inspection by most of his classmates. Alex noticed the women who continued to shine as the polish wore off the party girls and the fact that Daddy couldn't buy a real education sank in.

Alex knew that he noticed a different set of women than his peers and he was to set about, in his logical way, to get to know a few. He had spent the day walking around the grounds of the College Camp today to survey the prospects and had attempted to introduce himself to several of his new classmates.

For his efforts he had his participation in a game of Frisbee to show and the new knowledge that his self-perceived "cool" style with the ladies was no better than commonplace here at Baxter.

Alex had already realized that his college education would not take place exclusively in the classroom. And that his commitment to the logical course and a planned progression of things might be somewhat tested at Baxter.

CHAPTER THREE

...Like Steel It Was

As the day cooled at College Camp and the buses that would take the new class back to campus labored up the hill, the tug-of-war across the fire pond raged. And as it did, things began to get a little confused.

After all, how do you control such a mass effort? As the rope stretched across the corner of the pond, up the banks and over each side, the weight of those on the down slope proved too much for first one team and then the other. With much splashing and delighted screaming, the leaders of the new class and the followers who would be were pulled into the cool water. As the buses approached, the final victory for one of the teams became apparent.

A slow giving way grew into a mad rush to get out of the way as more and more weight was transferred to the down side of one bank. As the 150 or so students on the winning side backed up their bank, some small amount of slipping and sliding took place. As the rope and the young hands guiding it accelerated up and over the bank it took on a path and a course beyond the control of any one pair of those hands.

Amy, the girl with the hippie-style glasses and Alex the tall, serious looking boy were both part of the winning side in this final battle of the day. As the crowd moved up the bank, they did too. As Amy reached the crest of the bank, she slipped.

In an instant, without knowing quite how, she was under the rope! Somehow the rush had gotten ahead of her! As her side slammed into the mud and her now wet hair fell across her face she suddenly found that she was between the wet, muddy ground and the rope as it dragged across her shoulder and into her neck with the weight of seventy-five or eighty still screaming college freshmen! Now she screamed too.

The crowd of course didn't notice. They didn't see the one among them who was not screaming with glee. Nobody seemed to notice Amy and the rope dragging across and into her neck.

No one but Alex Clark noticed Amy Hudson and realized that her screaming wasn't like that of the others.

Now Alex discovered inadequacy.

His lanky, big boned, long-legged 190-pound frame was no match for the combined weight of his classmates. He watched as the rope dug into Amy's neck. He pulled with all his strength, realizing as he grabbed at it that the rope was like steel—that this malleable thing had become a steel cable—not about to give in to his efforts. He looked into Amy's eyes for the first time, looked at the expressive mouth and the wet, stringy hair hanging just down to the wet and hopelessly inadequate tee-shirt being pulled up to her shoulder. Alex's eyes met Amy's for the first time and he too screamed—screamed for his classmates not to kill this girl with the pleading in her eyes.

CHAPTER FOUR

...*It's Supposed To Be Easier Than This!*

Maybe it was her own screaming. Maybe it was that of Alex Clark. Probably it was just luck. The game ended and the rope slacked. As her classmates ran for the buses, Alex Clark helped Amy Hudson up, looked at the rope burns on her neck and pronounced them not serious.

Amy survived and the rope burns healed. The bruises eventually faded. That special spirit that was hers began to return even as she rode the bus home to the dorm with Alex's protective arm around her and that somewhat over dramatic look of concern and caring on his face. As she hunched against the window of the bus, shivering less from being cold and wet than from fear, her resolve to make changes hardened.

Amy survived and found that she enjoyed the attention Alex paid her in the days that followed. He visited her room often. He came around at almost every mealtime to see if she wanted to go along to the dining hall. It made her roommate a little jealous that this good-looking young man from upstairs would be spending all this time and attention on Amy. And Amy found that she enjoyed her roommate being annoyed.

Debbie resented more than anything how little effort Amy seemed to put into gaining Alex's attention. After all, what was so special about her? She certainly wasn't anything that special to look at.

Debbie looked in the mirror on the wall of the room she shared with Amy for the seventh time that hour, primped the wave in her blond hair, checked that her lipstick looked fresh and thought about her plain tomboy of a roommate.

Wouldn't you know these college geniuses would plant a low intensity bulb like Amy in with a high intensity spotlight like herself? Pleased with the comparison, she continued to ruminate about the paring of plain Amy and herself. She wondered if it would decrease the number of visitors like that Alex that sought out their room or whether it would just make Debbie look better by comparison. She ruffled the shaggy bangs dangling just the perfect way from her forehead with her long, painted nails and wondered again why Amy didn't try to look better.

Not that she couldn't be better with a little effort, she thought. Debbie was sure that a little eye shadow and some lip-gloss would do wonders. And those eyebrows! Hadn't this Upstater ever learned how to pluck and shape? Any woman knew, Debbie felt, that it took a little effort to make yourself look good. Debbie placed a lot of worth in looking her best and, if there had been much of a chance to meet Mister Right at beauty school, might have seriously considered it.

Mom had probably been right though, Debbie was deciding in that first week. "Use your attractiveness in a place where it might catch something worth having," she had said. "What you need is a place with real college men with real futures."

After surveying the available crop of college men, Debbie decided that she would do OK here. She guessed she could have done worse with roommates too. Amy was OK. She just wished she'd show a little interest in learning to make her self up. She seemed content with an almost tomboy look, most often in jeans and loose fitting tops. She seemed preoccupied with some task more important to her than trying to do something with that straight, pixie haircut.

"How about getting some priorities girl? There is more than classes and books to college. What about a social life?"

Amy enjoyed the attention Alex paid her and more so the concern he showed for her. He tried for a week to get her to the infirmary on campus to have her bruises and burns looked at and made clumsy excuses that his reason for visiting so often was just to check on her progress.

He seemed to really care one minute and then in the next, try to be the cool college man, on the make and after a conquest. It was an exciting and new game to Amy.

"Hey, how about going downtown with me tonight?" he'd say in his best Cool Man Clark, standing close and tall over her and then, as she looked disapprovingly at him—knowing that they were both still underage—and that at least *his* ID would never pass a close inspection, "No, I meant a movie!"

"Sure" she said, "I'd love to.

And the movie was fun as was the pizza that followed and the other things that filled those first couple of weeks. As they left the pizza shop, Alex tentatively took her hand. Amy immediately took his in her other hand, patted the back of his big paw and let go. She smiled up into his confused eyes, squinted that quizzical, questioning look at him and trotted toward the college's waiting shuttle bus.

The town was theirs to explore, new to both of them, as new to them as they were to college. As they explored, they leaned on each other. They each drew strength from the other as they tried new things.

Alex was drawn to her outward vulnerability and shared her desire to explore. Amy was drawn to his apparent strength and calm and confidence.

They explored the small college town, the movie house, the pizza and sub sandwich joints, found the bars their ID cards were good enough for, spoke to the merchants who welcomed the college kids each fall and learned to avoid those who didn't.

Amy and Alex learned to deal with the large numbers of people their own age too. Great in number and so similar in general appearance they found them to be diverse in their goals and aspirations. They talked about how superficial Debbie seemed to them and how mixed up Kevin—one of Alex's roommates—seemed. They drew on their by-chance friendship, concentrating on the things that made them alike and ignoring, for now, those that made them different.

October brought the colors to the trees and Alex managed to borrow a couple of bicycles. An entire Sunday was spent riding on young legs through the farm land and country hills that surrounded the college town.

A beautiful setting at a small bridge captivated them. Obviously evolved from one built not by the highway department but by the farmer who had owned the land, they found it by chance as they wandered the hills and broad valleys around Baxter. Along the curving dirt road leading up to the bridge on which they now paused, they found neatly trimmed grass that seemed to their eyes an especially silky shade of green.

A white farmhouse with broad porches and freshly painted dark green shutters sat at the bend in the road. An old, red barn sat across the road, its back doors open to the stream and the farmer's bottomland of recently harvested corn stalks. The curve in the road also allowed them to see the upper level doors to the barn, white painted Xs, bright in the sunshine, open to the ancient looking stone ramp facing the house across the road.

The colors of the leaves overhanging both roadway and stream shouted their peak brilliance as the afternoon sun shone through them and into the cool brook below. The old wooden bridge's solid feel beneath them seemed to perfect the scene. The wooden railing was painted the same brilliant white as the nearby farmhouse and the barn's trim. The wooden deck beneath their sneakered feet looked and felt as if it had been and would be there forever.

"It's so beautiful that it doesn't look real," Alex breathed.

"Uh-huh. It's hard to believe that the school is only a few miles over that hill," Amy agreed, panting slightly from the ride, gazing across the rolling farmland around them.

"I've done so much rushing around these past few weeks, that I think I've forgotten how peaceful a place like this can be."

"Huh? What's that," mumbled Amy, lost in her surroundings.

"Nothing, I'll tell you later."

As he looked at her now she wasn't the bookworm she claimed to be or the tomboy his roommates thought she was. She was free of this place and of the stress of school and fitting in. She looked happier now than he had seen her before. A little sweaty and flushed from the ride, she leaned over the railing, scoop neck of her blouse hanging loosely from her chest revealing gently cupped curves. Her freckled nose was just a little sunburned, straight hair hung across her cheeks. Her legs stretched out behind her cooling down from the ride.

Following the brook's path with her eyes, she appeared lost in the scene. She smiled that expressive smile at the rocks, the bubbling water and the leaves floating by in the gentle current.

She was suddenly much more than the tomboy or the bookworm he had befriended for the last month or so. He felt unexpected confusion rushing in.

CHAPTER FIVE

...Higher Education

Alex saw his friendship with Amy growing and was comfortable to use it to steady himself as he settled into college life. It was good to have Amy to drop in on when all was quiet and his studies bored him. It was reassuring to have someone to explore the town with. Amy was the perfect choice for his first college buddy he decided. Not as challenging as the guys on his floor, all trying to establish a place in the pecking order, but comfortable. Amy seemed perfect, he decided, because he had little to prove with her. She was safe, stable, and fit into his plan. And recently he could use some stability. Recently his plans for what college should be were suffering some stress.

The pecking order on the guy's floor was quick to be established. Even more so than in high school, your exploits, real or imagined by the crowd, established your place here. Some of the guys had established their 'rep' by letting it be known that their rooms were the place to get high. Some of those rooms, Alex decided, looked liked nothing else ever happened there but what came in the little pipes and the exotic-looking bongs.

Others established their places by showing how much they

could drink. Often they would seek to impress the others only to spend subsequent hours in the bathroom, praying to the porcelain god—paying for their daring. Alex had himself spent a couple of nights thusly occupied and was proud, in a strange feeling way, of the stature it now brought him on the floor—to be able to drink with the others without spilling his guts—as it were.

Still others claimed sexual exploits as their route to acceptance. One of the guys across the hall for instance, made it clear to a nice enough seeming girl from the floor below just exactly what he wanted for his birthday in mid-September. He then made it equally clear, after a night of drinking, friends shoving the two of them together and much giggling, that he had gotten 'it' exactly as requested. The girl's shy smile was seen by most as confirmation of the deed.

But the most confusing incident thus far had been when Mike, the other, more normal of Alex's two roommates, rushed in one mid-week night as Alex tried to fathom what was so damn important in the ramblings of one of the 'experts' in his sociology text.

"You'll never believe what's going on over on the girl's side."

"What now," Alex grumbled, "is Rick getting high right out in the hallway now?" referring to his growing annoyance with the clouds of pot smoke almost constantly emanating from the room next to theirs.

"No, but they're sure acting like it. He and Kevin are over there and man they are getting an eyeful. You know Sue, and Mindy and Carol's room?"

"Yeah, you mean that redhead whose always getting high with those guys?"

"Yeah, that's them, well they must be smoking some pretty good stuff this time because they're all over in the girls' room and Kevin and Rick just came out and said anyone can go over to visit that wants."

"So what?" sighed Alex, turning back to his text, hunching his shoulders as if to shut out this distraction.

"Well it just so happens that none of the girls are wearing any clothes. I swear, it's like a Playboy photo shoot over there!"

"Get out of here. I have to read this stuff for tomorrow. You're full of shit." Alex was learning quickly to modify his vocabulary to fit in with the guys even though Amy didn't seem to approve.

"No man, I swear it. Bobby is over there right now." Mike bounced up to the balls of his feet apparently eager to sprint back to the scene he was describing.

"This I gotta see!" Alex finally gave in, standing up and shoving the sociology anthology against the back of the study carrel. "Those girls are all great looking. What are they doing?"

"I don't know," Mike replied as they headed to the door, "something about just relaxing and what's the big deal, haven't any of you guys ever seen nude bodies before?"

"They *must* be stoned. Come on. Let's go."

Alex rushed along the corridor. Mike trailed along behind. Although eager to be a part of what was going on, Alex knew that Mike was so devoted to his girlfriend back home that he didn't feel right looking at other women. Alex correctly figured that Mike hoped to be part of the action by bringing Alex into it and hearing the details through him.

When they arrived at the girls' wing, there was a crowd of sorts already there. Five or six guys stood around in the hall, wanting too to be a part of the circus, but somehow intimidated by what might be behind the door that sat slightly ajar.

Alex hesitated for a moment too and then—not wanting to be left out if someone else gained the courage first—he elbowed his way toward the door. As he did, he thought of the stories his cousin had told him of his time at Baxter and thought that this might prove that the era of free love that Ted had lived through at college was not past after all.

It had not been evident from his brief experience but perhaps this was the start. He pushed the door open a little more and stuck his head into the room.

"Hey, what's going on guys?"

Alex immediately sounded awkward—even to himself—realizing that he had no legitimate reason to be there if challenged. He felt rather more naked than those he found in the room.

In the room sat Rick, his neighbor, the drug supply for the floor, clothed as usual in long-fringed suede jacket, jeans and boots. Next to him sat Kevin, Alex's other, transfer-aged roommate. Three years older than both Mike and Alex, he looked more like he should be playing guitar with a southern rock band than playing college student. In long blond hair, droopy mustache and flowered shirt hanging out of his patched and faded jeans, his priorities at college were not immediately clear.

These two were both sitting near the door on desk chairs—grinning—eyes just happy slits, obviously high.

On the lower bunk lay Carol Addams, a stunningly ample blond whose long tresses and ready smile had already made her popular around the campus. She lay under a comforter, bare shoulders showing and giving clues to what else she wasn't wearing under the blanket. Across from her, on a cushioned lounge chair 'borrowed' from the floor's TV lounge, half illuminated by the glow of the only light source in the room, a lava lamp of all things, lounged Mindy Cohen, with Sue Morgan curled up at her feet on the carpet. Both of these women obviously wore nothing at all.

They lounged with the ease and relaxed nature that Alex had come to recognize in Kevin after he had been next door getting high with Rick. They seemed to care about little at the moment except enjoying the sensation they were creating.

All three women were beautiful, yet each strikingly different. Alex had earlier wondered aloud to Mike—now at the door, stretching his neck to see around him—how the College had found the foresight to place three such beautiful women together in the same room.

Where Mindy was dark, with jet black hair and long sensuous legs, Sue had dark red hair of fire that kinked down her back like a mane and the freckles typical of redheads now showing themselves to be not confined strictly to her face, arms and legs.

"Hey man, we're just hanging around," leered Rick, a knowing wink coming from his glassy eyes.

"Yeah, close the door Alex," added Kevin.

Again Alex hesitated, feeling naked. He both wished that he could close the door and join the others and knew that if he did, he could do nothing but stare stupidly.

The girls were in control. The three men in the room, and those out in the hall, were permitted to be there, to dream, to fantasize but to touch only if some, yet to be negotiated, further permission was granted

They were all on the same wavelength, be it a marijuana induced one or some new college rite Alex did not understand. He could obviously do nothing but intrude.

"What's the matter Alex, never seen skin before," taunted Mindy as he hesitated, grasping for something to say.

"I...I, was just looking for Kevin," unable to even look at the women now.

"Yeah, what's the matter," said Carol from the bed, disappointment in her voice and obviously not as stoned as the others. "What do you think this is some kind of freak show?"

She pulled the blanket higher up around her, tired of the game her roommates had dragged her into. She was disappointed that Alex, who she had suggested inviting to the little gathering, was reacting so awkwardly.

Although she had noticed Alex around the hall and had been looking for an excuse to meet the tall, serious freshman, now she was embarrassed to see his awkwardness. When her roommates and Rick and Kevin had suggested this little expression of freedom and open-mindedness, she had hoped that it would make it easier to make friends. Shy, despite her full figure and stunning looks, she had felt overshadowed by the more aggressive Mindy and Sue since her arrival at Baxter. Baxter was big compared to her previous school and she felt lost here.

Now she felt exposed despite the blanket. She felt the leering boys out in the hall and the stammering Alex would now be even harder to get to know. The spectacle was backfiring and she saw new walls going up.

"I, I'm, uh, sorry, I, uh, didn't know," he lied. "I was just looking for Kevin for something…it can wait."

He pushed out the door, through the others now crowding behind him and hurried back to his room.

"That was really dumb. What are those idiots trying to prove?" He flew at Mike when he returned a few minutes later.

God, it was all supposed to be easier than this he thought as he reopened the sociology book and tried weakly to digest what he had just seen, the face he had lost by bungling into it and the teaching of the scholars whose articles appeared in the book.

Dissonance, alienation—his text spoke of these things in cold, clinical terms. Alex realized that he was feeling his own version. The world was supposed to make sense. If you did your best and took careful steps toward your goals, life was supposed to reward you with things that made sense. Why then, Alex wondered, did these incongruities keep rearing up at him? What was it that kept confronting him with things that didn't fit, that shouldn't be—that confused him?

Sociology told him that society was becoming more complex and therefore less meaningful to the individual. His head told him that if he stuck to his plan, fulfillment and security would result.

His heart wasn't so sure. He buried his confusion under yet another layer of seriousness and returned to his studies.

CHAPTER SIX

...*Changes at Quail Brook*

Now on the wooden railed bridge, the confusion of that night came flooding back.

College was supposed to be merely the next step in his plans, the next step to med. school, a job, and his future. But the struggle of coping with the unexpected diversity of college muddled the plan.

He didn't have time to waste on drugs but his roommate seemed intent on shoving them down his throat. Booze in appropriate doses lubricated his self-confidence but that lubrication came at a price. And the jarring taunt of Carol Addams still rang in his ears. College women left him with many more questions than answers. Why was he left feeling so uncomfortable around them just when his plans called for different priorities right now? He had a purpose, a place to go.

Only Amy's friendship had been reassuring. She had been a constant through this turbulent first couple of months. She had been a friend, someone to talk to. She was too much of a tomboy to be threatening like the flashy girls at the frat parties or the teasing, stoned girls back at the residence hall. Amy was too accepting to confuse him—at least very often.

But now there was that far away look in her eye. The same look that he had seen when, with a rope stretched between them, he first looked into those brown, innocent yet knowing eyes.

That look spoke of a purpose beyond his plans. That look spoke of meeting life's challenges head on.

There was no rope between them now and again Alex felt naked—his planned, orderly, safe course stripped away from him as she turned toward him.

She felt it too apparently, smiling her most expressive, inquiring smile.

"Romantic, isn't it?" she asked.

Angered that his confusion should be so easy to see, angered that Amy, of all people, would be the cause of it, Alex fumbled for something to say.

"It's OK, I guess."

And then, unable to stop himself, not wanting to stop himself, tingling with fear of the line he crossed as he did it, he reached for her and kissed her. She responded willingly. It was a long kiss, as romantic as he could make it. He felt her in his arms for the first time, felt her breasts lean in against his chest and the curve of her hip under his hand. He felt his own arousal welling up and was sure that she would feel it too, an arousal that surprised him, confused him even more.

They broke the embrace and she said, pushing her hair back across her forehead and letting it fall casually, apparently much more in control than he, "Well, that was unexpected."

Liar! He felt like shouting. He could actually feel his nostrils flare and his cheeks redden. He felt trapped and tricked out of the last simple friendship he had had! How dare she be so calm!

"What brought that on?" she continued with just the hint of a smile at the corner of that expressive mouth.

Alex struggled with his anger. Anger at himself, anger at her and anger at the emotions that dominated the way he found himself thinking about Amy. He stalked across the bridge to the other railing and back.

"You said it was a romantic spot," he said feeling the last sheltered part of his changing world slipping away, "I just thought we should try it out".

He took one last look at the brook peacefully burbling at their feet and mounted his borrowed bike, feeling rather more heated that the afternoon temperature called for.

"Let's go," he said, "It's getting late."

She smiled at him, smiled to herself, shrugged and followed into the afternoon sunlight.

CHAPTER SEVEN

...*Should Have Been*

Alex had seemed to be struggling with himself. He seemed to be at war with some inner demon that kept him from letting go, from experiencing all of what the moment held. His confusion amused Amy because she was obviously at least partly the cause of it. This was a new experience for her and she relished the power she felt. She had never been able to cause this kind of struggle in a boy before. Like all her new experiences since arriving at Baxter though, it excited her.

Amy was lying on her bed, taking advantage of a rare moment of quiet on the hallway, the day after the big bike excursion. She thought back over her college own initiations.

Since her first terrifying brush with danger in September, she had found herself more and more energized by the possibilities of college life. College seemed to offer unlimited possibilities for reinventing oneself. Although her roommate and most of the other girls around her saw attracting and getting to know guys as the most natural thing in the world, for Amy it was a new experience. While Debbie spent time primping for the men in her life and then teasing them into insanity, Amy sought mainly to conquer her fear *of* them.

Alex had been the first college man she had met and the dramatic way that they had met endeared him to her. She accepted this and enjoyed the friendship that developed.

Alex seemed kind and concerned for her while she recovered from the rope burns and bruises received at College Camp but seemed unable to relax around her. He always seemed possessed by a need to do the right thing, to say the right thing. Just when she thought he was relaxing, he would say something canned or corny.

Amy lay on her stomach, kicking her feet slowly back and forth behind her, propped up on her elbows just enough to see over the windowsill and into the quad in front of the dorm if she chose. She smiled to a song quietly coming from Debbie's Marantz amplifier and continued to muse.

Alex seemed to need order in his life. He seemed to fear letting loose and experiencing anything off his chosen path. His fear of straying into the unknown she took as something they had in common. She saw this as the basis of their friendship.

His unwillingness to face his fears though, she saw as a weakness and it had so far kept them from being any more to each other than friends to spend time and explore with.

Amy understood fear. She had feared almost everything for almost as long as she could remember. She began though, to see her chance to face those fears at college. Although she feared all that she was experiencing, she began to get a kind of rush from it. The more she explored the things that scared her, the more alive she felt. Each new experience seemed to give her new energies to draw upon. Each new encounter seemed to reduce the fear she felt and make her more powerful in the balance. Amy began to feel in control of her own life.

"Amy, I need the room tonight." Debbie had said when Amy returned from the library one night.

"What do you mean?" she asked naively.

"Robby is in there," Debbie had whispered, blocking the door "and I think he's going to spend the night. Come on, be a friend!"

"But what about my stuff?" Amy indicated the bundle in her arms. "Where am I supposed to sleep?"

Amy argued briefly but she had already felt that rush of excitement, wishing it was she who was kicking her roommate out, she that was going to share her bed with someone tonight.

"Why don't you go stay upstairs with Alex?" Debbie persisted.

That would really throw him, Amy thought briefly. But her tall friend would never be comfortable with something like that unless he had planned it. Amy agreed to sleep in a neighbor's room but tingled through the night as she lie on the floor in a borrowed sleeping bag, thinking about what was happening in her own room.

The next day Debbie had seemed different. She was somehow even more self-assured and confident. She and Robby started spending all their time together and Amy was left again with her fears and, more than ever, with her longing to conquer them.

The college social scene soon gave her the chance she sought. There were enough parties for which no invitation was needed to begin with and after a while the invitations started coming of their own accord.

Amy found that beer didn't seem to have much effect on her. She never got sick like so many others around her and she certainly wasn't about to be a part of some of the drunken antics that passed for fun at these parties. She did however feel more relaxed around people after drinking a couple and as she became more relaxed she became better at relaxing.

The more she went to parties and interacted with her peers, the less it threatened her. It soon became easier to deal with other people, including men. Her fears seemed to fade away somewhat and this excited her. By early October, she was dragging other girls to the parties in the building.

Usually dressed in jeans and a simple blouse, no make-up and her glasses, she didn't exactly have to fight the guys off at first but when they did make advances, more and more often now, she learned to play with the excitement within herself. Dressing more in ways that she learned would encourage the game and perfecting the sly twinkle in her eye and her inviting smile as assets, she began to debate with herself whether this one or that one would be OK to take back to her room to kick Debbie out for the night. The boys seemed to enjoy the game as much as she but none had yet made their way successfully back to the room. In none of them had she yet seen what it would take to win that thrilling argument within her.

She focused on her own image in the darkening glass of her window for a moment. Freckled, pug-nosed, straight hair, yet, for the first time really, she began to feel some pride in who she was and what she was about. Classes were easy. It was life that was the challenge.

She longed to take control of her life. She longed to take new risks, to try those things that had always scared her. She loved the power she felt playing the social game she was learning but the thoughtful outcast within her hesitated at the shallowness of mere conquest without feeling.

Now things finally seemed to be fitting themselves into place. The long October ride with Alex in the hot Indian summer sun had led them to the perfect spot. The tree-shaded brook with the little bridge over it had been all she could have dreamed.

She had realized then and there that Alex Clark should be the one to take back to her room. She was surprised that she hadn't seen it long before. It seemed only natural that she would make this serious boy who had tried so gallantly to save her life her first lover.

The thrill of this realization had been almost overwhelming. It had filled her with energy and excitement. She had leaned across the railing of the bridge and looked into the water below, seeing her fears float down stream with the autumn leaves and knowing that the only way to conquer them was to live them. She knew the excitement of the unplanned, the new and different. She took her glasses off and smiled at Alex.

CHAPTER EIGHT

The Trouble with Challenging Your Fears...

Amy and Alex's romantic interlude on Farmer Simpson's bridge over Quail Brook ended as suddenly as it began. Alex practically fled the pretty autumn scene on his borrowed bicycle, claiming to suddenly realize how late it was getting and that he had lots of studying to do. Amy followed and they rode back to campus in the lengthening shadows. They didn't become lovers that night in Amy's room either. Debbie didn't have to find another place to sleep that night or for quite a few subsequent nights. Lost in his flight from confusion and in her conflict between the rush of the new and the fear of the different, they were unable to find each other.

Amy took another young man to be her first lover, a soccer player who belonged to the athletes' fraternity and was enamored of her spunky attitude and perky smile. He was macho and always smiling. Large and broad-shouldered with a shock of black hair splayed across his forehead, he treated her like a doll, tossing her around when playing and encircling her protectively with a hairy arm when they were watching a movie or hanging out in the campus Rathskeller. Amy helped him with his math and biology and he helped her with her self-confidence.

They became regulars together at the parties and after a few weeks, his foreplay got more serious. Finally, one lazy Saturday afternoon just after midterms, as they lay around in her room reading, Debbie away for the weekend, he playfully rolled on top of her. They kissed and as his hands ran up and down the sides of her, she knew it was time.

It was different than she had expected, more intense and rushed. She cataloged every sensation, gave herself in to every feeling. Lost in the sweaty motion, a little surprised when it was over, she collapsed into his arms listening to his heavy breathing.

She was thrilled and excited as she knew now she would be every time she challenged her fears. Max's reckless style appealed to her and the abandon with which he attacked life fed her desire for the rush of adrenaline that challenges brought.

While the relationship with him lasted only a month or so longer, she had now learned to attack life when it scared her. She vowed that from now on she would center on the things that scared her most and *do* them. Do them and prove that she could. She vowed never to be afraid of herself.

Alex ran for the cover of a less challenging existence. He buried himself in his school work, in the Baxter basketball team and a nice normal girl. According to plan, Katie had materialized. A cheerleader for the team, she was long and thin and blond. A winning smile first attracted him and the genuineness behind that smile kept his interest. As he got to know her, after practice or a game, they found that they had much in common. Both saw Baxter as on the way to something greater. Both were looking for a relationship without too many complications. Both were happy to simply be what the other needed at the time.

She had been a natural choice and she became his steady girl. His life returned to normal for a while. The confusion of those first several weeks of adjustment was over. Carving out a little corner for himself, he bought into his part of the college experience. He learned to cope with the vagrancy of college life and the constant assault of new things, experiences and ideas. If he observed them, considered them and chose without haste—those that fit into his plan for life—college wasn't that bad after all.

TWO

SUMMER

A Little Later

CHAPTER NINE

A Montezuma Sunset...

The sunset is an incredible orange ball on the horizon. Around it, there is nothing to obstruct the view. Circles of red fading into blue, into an aqua green, fading into purple, into the blue black of night, against the roof of this big, big sky.

Until seen, a person who has grown up surrounded by the East's rolling hills and valleys can't fully imagine the vastness of the sky out here. With mile after mile of flat, level, unbroken land stretching on either side of the highway, the sky is a full 180 degrees from horizon to horizon.

Easterners and city dwellers only see a fraction of the sky. They are so hemmed in by mountains or trees or streetlights or buildings that they only see parts of the sky among all those obstacles. Out here, it is a completely different story. The difference is very hard to describe to someone who has not seen it or experienced it. The abruptness with which the scenery changes from the sharp, unfriendly hills of Western Pennsylvania to the flat corn fields of Illinois, to the untamed rolling hills of Eastern Kansas, to these seemingly endless, flat plains of South Western Kansas has to be experienced to be understood.

Lights dot the Western horizon and a town rises up, out of the plain. A sudden cluster of trees announce the arrival as they mark, I now know, the luxury of shade, reserved for the homes that mark, in turn, another whistle stop for the A & T & Santa Fe rail cars that race us down Route 56.

Montezuma, Kansas the water tower proclaims as we rattle past the John Deere dealer's lights, the 'D & D Rest. and Bar' and the ever present grain elevators.

Those elevators are the most distinguishing feature of this beautiful and lonely landscape—taller by far than any other structure and more descriptive in their utilitarian design and function, than the squat homes tucked in under the water-thirsty trees. The elevators take on an eerie look as the sun sinks behind them. They are like sentinels guarding the little town so remote from the eastern hills of my childhood. The little clusters of trees flash by as we pass the little towns like Montezuma, scattered along the thin strip of concrete Jack and I now follow.

Boy, if Alex could only see me now. This adventure would rock his little, planned-out world to its foundations. Riding across the country in this big Cabover Pete would frazzle him. It still terrifies me I guess. Tall and square and white as snow, the cab punches a monstrous hole in the wind as we race along. Sleek and silver, the trailer follows along obediently behind us.

Our Peterbilt is the muscle and the brains of our operation. The trailer is the beast of burden. Our cab sits high to allow the engine to be mounted directly under our seats and between the front wheels. The view from the giant, wrap-around windscreen makes you feel powerful and in control. With no hood sticking out in front like the more traditional cab-behind-the-engine configuration, you feel like you are on the edge of a cliff at first. You see all that glass and nothing but road beyond it. Sitting directly on the turning wheels, the pivot caused by the turn of the big wheel is different than in a car and that also takes some getting used to.

The sleeper behind you though gives you a feeling of security. Your home on the road, it is always there and waiting. Whenever the road or the weather or the hours get to be too much, the sleeper allows a re-charge.

The sky darkens and Montezuma fades behind us. With it and with these musings for company, my fears fade as well. How could anyone blame a girl for being a little apprehensive, the way this trip started out? But the wealth of experiences I'm saving up now energizes me. They help me to do more and more. Alex is probably somewhere back in Westchester, working at some boring little job, planning methodically for the next semester, the next step in his plan. Well, I hope he reaches all his goals— becomes that doctor he wants to be. I'll always love him for what and who he is—different from me but OK in his own way. Just wait 'til we get back to Baxter in the fall and I tell him about *my* summer.

CHAPTER TEN

...The Big Ride

The first part of the trip had been easy. A salesman had provided the first, easy hop across New York State from Baxter. Reassured by his quiet manner and his fatherly admonishments against hitchhiking, Amy had been put somewhat at ease. He drove smoothly and with a nonchalance that was contagiously relaxing but his rumpled gray suit and tired, dark-circled eyes tipped her off that what he was looking for was someone to talk to and someone to keep him awake until his next stop. Amy settled quickly into the desired role of Listener and Monitor, asking questions when ever his attention seemed to flag and by the end of their four hours together both emerged refreshed from their time together.

"My name is Amy Hudson." she'd started out politely, "Where are you headed?"

"I'm Bill Swinski," he had replied, don't you know that hitchhiking is dangerous?"

"That's why I'm doing it, to find out if I should be afraid."

He rolled his eyes and smiled. He shifted his weight a little more toward the door and began to banter playfully with the young girl about the wisdom of doing things you know to be dangerous.

Baxter had been changed dramatically when a girl had been abducted that past winter while hitchhiking. The girl, a freshman like Amy, had accepted a ride from someone just to get from downtown to campus, just like dozens of the college students in Baxter did every day.

She had not been heard from again until the snows melted and she was found in a shallow grave in the hills across the valley from Baxter. Her alleged killer and rapist had been caught and was now awaiting trial, but the effect on Baxter and on its college and its students would be a long time wearing off.

For most, the fear induced by the experience of losing a classmate made them more cautious and less adventuresome. For Amy Hudson, it drove her to quiet determination. Unwilling to let this warning rob her of new found freedom and confidence, she attacked what she feared, hitching a ride to a concert in Binghamton in the weeks that followed Lisa Henderson's disappearance and, at the end of her spring term, hitching across the state to visit her cousin in Buffalo.

Amy arrived at her Cousin Becky's eager and energized. Although she had begun this trip with a fear that every ride would end up offered by a killer or a rapist, her across-the-state introduction had calmed those fears. Amy's plans for the summer solidified and she had shared them with Becky.

"I'm going to hitchhike to California and back," she told Becky. "I'm going to face as many of my fears as I can and I'm going to push myself like I've never done before."

"But what will your folks say?" Becky challenged, "They'll never go along with something that crazy!"

Amy had explained the plan. She'd tell her folks and Becky's mom that she'd take the bus to California and, depending on what happened once there, she'd tell her father's sister in Los Angeles that she'd be taking the bus to her next destination, whatever that turned out to be.

"Look," she explained, "hasn't it already worked this far? Your mom and my mom both think I took a bus from Baxter to here, don't they?"

Becky thought about this for a while and then said matter of factly, "I'm coming too."

"Oh no," countered Amy, This is something I have to do by myself."

Becky eventually understood and reluctantly agreed to the conspiracy as the plans were discussed and refined late into the night.

Those first easy rides and the ease with which her parents were willing to accept her supposed bus trip drove her further. Parents too old to know better and too tired to care very much suddenly became an asset, and after a week with her cousin in Buffalo, Amy was ready for her real summer adventure. Not only did she need to confront her fears and apprehensions about hitchhiking by doing it, she needed to conquer them. Amy therefore embarked on her cross-country trip—by bus as far as her parents knew and by thumb in reality.

The first rides out of Buffalo had been uneventful and if not for the newness of it all and the countryside to see, would have been boring. The families traveling for the summer, the locals good for only a few miles and the older men looking for permission to leer as payment for the ride, moved her along and continued to boost her confidence. Her legs, displayed audaciously for her, by short, summer cutoff jeans, her light, closer fitting now, tee-shirts and her now longer wavy hair, ensured her enough attention along the road to guarantee rides and to make the trip even more thrilling for her.

Her first ride in an eighteen-wheel truck had been disappointing. She had perhaps anticipated too much. She had watched those huge, powerful, and to her glorious, behemoths rush past with such purpose and force that she eagerly climbed up the first time one slowed and stopped for her. When situated next to the driver, she was awed at the height and vastness of the cab and thrilled with her success. As the truck slowly gained speed and re-entered traffic the driver drawled "Where you goin' Missy?" out of the side of his mouth and spit brown tobacco juice into a little can he cradled on his lap. He leered as devilishly as the worst of the salesman types had and commenced to banter with her throughout the ride. Unlike her tired salesman friend though, this banter consisted mainly of barely veiled suggestions about his lonesomeness, her legs and the relief that he sought as payment for the ride.

"Where ya goin' Honey," he leered again, looking her over from head to toe. "Nice tan you're gettin' their sweetie."

"Looks like you're ready for a ride with a man."

"Those shorts shrink in the wash?" "Come on, let Ol' Buster see what you got there, huh?" "What's a matter, cat got your tongue?"

"I just need a ride to the next rest stop," Amy had said, "My boyfriend is waiting for me there."

"Must not be much of a boyfriend to let you loose like this." Buster continued. "Maybe I can show you how a real man can take care of those legs for you."

"Just a ride to the next rest area please," Amy strained to sound calm, "My boyfriend if waiting for me and he worries a lot."

"The next stop is right up here in Kimball, is that where this big man is?"

"Yes, his name is Alex and he works there at the gas pumps," she lied, "Maybe you've seen him before. He's a real big guy, used to be a boxer. He's got a real bad temper too. Have you ever met him?"

Amy made that ride as short as possible and hid in the women's rest room for nearly an hour to make sure he had gone when she talked him into stopping at the rest area outside of Kimball, Ohio.

Although she wondered for a while if her trip had been such a great idea, she remained determined to face her fears as they presented themselves. Although she wished the real Alex was around now and then when she needed him, she soon set out again, this time with a nice enough looking family in a van and within hours was once again trying to pick up a ride from an eighteen-wheeler.

CHAPTER ELEVEN

Warehouse Billy...

Chicago is where the trip turned serious. Amy had been riding all afternoon with a big, husky kid of a driver headed for a warehouse on the south side of the city. He seemed young and clean and not really smart enough to be a danger so when he suggested that he could take her right on to St. Louis after making his pick-up in Chicago, she went along with it. Billy bragged endlessly that his big Kenworth was the best that money could buy and proudly showed Amy what all the buttons and levers did. He shocked her with the price he had paid for the big shiny rig and told her long stories about his new wife back in New Hampshire. He talked about how, even with the big truck's loan payment, they planned to be able to save up enough to get out of their trailer and into a real house in only a few years. His wife's father had been in trucking for years when he had had his heart attack and it seemed natural for the new son-in-law to use his established credit to obtain the new "K-whopper".

Amy listened to it all intently. She drank up the details of this alien lifestyle. Away from his wife for a week at a time, Billy claimed that they would park the big rig behind the trailer upon his return and spend all the next day in bed before checking in on her folks across the street and reporting back to the company for another run. Billy seemed to enjoy telling his rider about his life immensely and it fascinated Amy. He patted the picture of his plump, smiling bride, rubber banded to the visor above his head and smiled at Amy. "Stay Safe and Come Home to My Loving Lips, Jackie" was scribbled across the bottom of the picture. The smoothness of the ride, the power of all that height and rolling weight captivated her. Billy seemed harmless enough, so she agreed to continue on to St. Louis after his pick-up in Chicago.

It was raining when they rolled into the warehouse yard at nine p.m. It didn't occur to Amy that the dock might be shut down. She was so engrossed in the stories Billy told she hardly noticed the instructions of the guard to park down in the yard until the dock opened up the next morning. Only when Billy shut the big rig down did she begin to come out of it. Although she had accepted his offer of a continued ride, the prospect of spending the night in this fenced in yard with hardly another truck in sight and absolutely no other people around made her a little nervous.

Schooled a little now in the jargon of the rider's world, she asked Billy if he expected payment for the ride. When he replied that there were no free rides, she was suddenly faced with a vision of Lisa Henderson's picture in the newspaper back in Baxter. She tried to calm herself.

'Come on girl', she said to herself, balling her hands into fists beside her until it hurt. 'This is exactly the fear you're supposed to be conquering. What's the matter with you? Why so suddenly nervous?' Her heart beat loudly in her chest and her eyes looked inward as well as at Billy.

Her instincts had been right. Billy had expected payment and had considered it just a natural part of the deal. All the stories about wife Jackie back in New Hampshire and the father-in-law across the street hadn't meant that the ride should be free. It turned out that Billy's father-in-law had given him more than schooling in the mechanics of trucking. He had also taught him that the way to survive the long nights away from home was to find 'it' where you could. As long as Billy kept coming home to his baby daughter, whatever action he could scare up along the way was just fine—just proved he was a man with needs after all.

Although very matter of fact about it all, Billy's expectations didn't exactly meet with Amy's. It had been a long night. There had been considerable arguing.

"Come on Honey, give it up for Billy-Boy, he had started as soon as the rig was secured and he had checked to see that no one else seemed to be paying much attention.

"Oh, Billy," she tried, fighting to sound calm, "think about Jackie."

"You know, your Father-in Law was wrong, it's really best when you wait for it."

"Does your Mother-in Law know what you do when you're on the road?" "What would she and Jackie say if they knew what you are asking of me?" She fought to sound cool, tried to remain nonchalant, tried to joke him out of it; all the time hearing a sound like rushing water in her ears.

"So you want to be a fighter, huh?" Billy seemed turned-on by her reaction. "Where you gonna go little Amy?" "It's raining pretty hard out there now and this here sleeper is about the only dry place you're gonna be finding tonight. I guess I won't mind a little fight for my reward; guess I could use the work out." His eyes narrowed and his voice dropped to a steely growl. "What's it gonna be girl," he continued, serious yet with a light of excitement in his eyes, "rough or easy?"

"OK Billy, if that's what you want, I know the rules," she breathed, matching his lowered tone, "I can live with myself, if you can."

He smiled and relaxed a bit. "That's better."

Amy found herself using the 'I need a bathroom' trick again. "Please Billy, I have to go first," she lied. She crossed her legs and wiggled a little for effect. "I'll meet you in the sleeper but first I have to find a bathroom."

"Oh damn it all," he grumbled, obviously already worked up for what he felt was coming to him, "over there," indicating a dim light at the end of the loading dock.

Amy jumped down quickly from the cab. She trotted across the lot in the rain to the long, dark loading dock and looked back at Billy's Kenworth. He sat illuminated by the cab lights, watching her and unbuttoning his flannel shirt. She scurried in the direction of the dimly lit Rest Room sign.

Inside, she was faced with a dirty, wet room with dirty, wet facilities. Wet herself now, she faced her situation, grateful for this slim chance. Rain or no rain, she had to get out of here. She edged over to the door and surveyed the parking lot. Sitting in a depression, near the railroad tracks, it was lit only by a couple of spotlights on the edge of the building's roof. Pitch dark, except for right in front of the dock, where the trucks backed up each morning, it was fenced all around.

The two other trucks in the lot were quiet and dark. She saw no help there. Barbed wired along the top of the fence glinted in the rain and spotlights. The only way out was past the guardhouse at the top of the hill. She looked back at the baby blue Kenworth. Billy appeared to have climbed in back to await her return. Glad that he seemed to be confirming her first evaluation of his intelligence, she put her head down, hitched her wet knapsack over her shoulder, and sprinted into the dark. She scooted past the guard station and the dozing guard as quietly as she could and ran into the rainy night.

Amy spent what seemed like hours staying in the shadows and walking until she finally found her way back to the interstate. She was pretty wet and bedraggled when a car full of drunken kids about her own age but with apparently far fewer worries picked her up at the bottom of the ramp. They drove too fast for the rainy weather but were eager for her to join them at their next port of call; a club called the NeveRest. She followed as far as the door to the noisy roadhouse and then faded back as her rescuers melted in to the crowd.

She walked to a Motel Six along the edge of the interstate and spent most of her last $36.00 on a dry room.

Her escapes that night had been affected, more than anything else, by using the same vulnerable and pitiful waif-like look that she had learned to use on football players at school who, after too long at the beer tap, had cornered her. She had become so good at turning that look of innocence and vulnerability on and off that Billy had seemed to hesitate a little before pressing for his ride payment. She had turned it on full force to get him to let her out of the truck to find a bathroom. Alex had dubbed this her "Hungry Waif" look and she was grateful now for the security it now seemed to bring her.

In spite of the rain and her fear, her confidence continued to grow.

CHAPTER TWELVE

...Glorious!

She absolutely swaggered into the diner. She smiled at each driver as he looked up at her. Her mood could not be diminished, even by the wink of the Counter Man to several of the other drivers or the sniff of indignation of the waitress.

She had driven the Peterbilt into the lot. She had climbed down from the Driver's side and led Jack into the "Professional Drivers Only" section of the Lazy-R Truck Stop diner.

After the close call with Billy in the warehouse yard and a couple of long and wet nights in Chicago, Amy had finally hooked up with Jack Menand just east of St. Louis. Looking pretty bedraggled by then and fearing the ultimate failure of her cross-country plans, she was surprised that this slight, balding, middle-aged man had even bothered to pick her up.

"Goin West?" was all he had asked and "Might as well ride along." was all the explanation he had offered for violating company policy and offering the young girl a ride.

When the excitement of being on the move again wore off, the St. Louis Arch was behind them and the lack of sleep the past few days had brought began to catch up with her, Amy had found herself slumped against the door, head rattling along on the window.

"Get on up there, you'll be more comfortable", was all Jack had said, gesturing to the double sleeper on the back of his cab when a bump in the road brought her momentarily back awake. She had gratefully complied and slept soundly in his private home on the road, feeling somehow safe and secure with this little man of few words.

Hours later she had barely noticed when the truck finally stopped and had not even responded to the tingle of fear she felt when Jack had dropped into the far side of the sleeper's bed beside her.

It was very natural. Jack kept driving west and Amy kept watching and asking questions. At night, sleeping in the cab next to Jack was both exciting and safe. While still a little scary, it was thrilling for the success it brought. The adventure was finally succeeding. She found herself jumping at the chance when Jack called, a week after he had dropped her off at her Aunt's house in California, politely and as always, with few words, to "see if you wouldn't like to ride along again" on his next trip east?

Amy called her Mother from the hall phone with her Aunt Daisy listening from her spot by the kitchen sink. As it began to ring, she depressed the hook and the call disconnected.

She spoke into the phone as if to her Mother, described the weather, her trip to the Zoo and shopping with her Aunt. She told the dead phone that she would be boarding a bus for the return trip in a day or two and that she might stop in Phoenix to see a school friend on the way home. She promised to call again soon and hung up the receiver.

The next day, her Aunt dropped her off at the bus station with admonishments about strangers and cautionaries about the people you meet in bus stations. Amy thanked her, insisted that she not go to the trouble of waiting, and hitched her knapsack once again onto her shoulder. She pushed through the double doors, a confident world traveler.

As soon as she was sure that her Aunt had turned the corner, she was back at the curb. In a few minutes a pale yellow Maverick chugged around the opposite corner and the little man of few words pushed open the passenger door.

Jack smiled when he saw her and said, "Now we'll have to do an extra little shuffling to make this work, lady."

Amy nodded and listened to his instructions. No overt greeting was called for. No hugs and 'thank you for coming', no 'I'm so excited about being asked to come along', was appropriate, just a small Ford picking up a brown-haired girl with a knapsack.

No longer afraid, Amy thought.

Amy walked slowly along the south Los Angeles street. She had just passed the gate into the big B & R Depot. There seemed to be hundreds of big rigs like Jack's pulling up to the neatly lined up trailers, backing slowly under the fifth wheel hook-ups and connecting for their trips to wherever. The tractor/cabs were all different, the colors and stripes indicating the individual style and preferences of their owners. Some had names painted on the noses and a whirlwind of stripes and colors. Some had multiple antennae and deflectors and windcheaters. Others, like Jack's, were simple white with a stripe designed to match the company trailer it most consistently pulled (yellow in Jack's case). There were Kenworths and Peterbilts, Whites and Internationals, all with owner/operator names on the driver's doors and below the logo of the company who had financed them.

The trailers, on the other hand, were all the same. Clean and white with the huge lettering and logo of the trucking firm advertising 'On-Time Coast to Coast" down each side, they passed one by one out of the gates where Jack had dared not take her.

A truck rumbled past and she looked up in time to see it was a maroon Kenworth. Another followed, this time a white Peterbilt.

She thought it looked like Jack's rig but, following instructions, she steadfastly held her pace and resisted the temptation to wave. The big trucks turned a corner together two blocks down and Amy's heart sank as she began to suspect that Jack had had a change of heart and would not be stopping for her as they had planned. She walked three, then four more blocks. She was now well beyond where she had seen most of the B & R Trucks turning toward the interstate.

Amy started to plan her next move in her head. Maybe it was just too risky for Jack to stop for her after all. Maybe he had just realized that he was being foolish for inviting a teenager to ride across the country with him. Well OK, she'd head for the interstate herself and begin hitching again. Maybe she'd head north this time. She'd heard that Seattle was nice and that San Francisco was really the place to find your freedom.

Lost in thought, having moved on in her mind to the next adventure, she paid little attention to the noise of a tractor-trailer coming up behind her as she walked. Only when the air brakes hissed and squeaked did she look up to Jack completing the plan. He stopped only long enough for her to jump aboard and immediately swung the truck back into the light morning traffic.

"Sorry," he said, "had to lose that other rig before I could come back for you."

Amy just smiled and settled back into the passenger chair.

The double sleeper on the back of his Peterbilt insulated them from the world outside; kept reasonably warm by the idling truck engine and the padded insulation that also kept out most of the truck and road noise from outside, Amy felt safe there. Never pushed or pressured by her gentlemanly guide, she soon began to look at the cab as their own private home.

Three weeks later on their fourth ride together, forty-five year old Jack Menand quietly became eighteen year old Amy's lover.

As was becoming their custom, the day had been as quiet as it was beautiful. Hours on the desert road led them into that sudden western darkness that Amy had quickly come to love. The traffic on I-40 thinned out until it seemed that the truckers had it all to themselves. Gradually even the overland carriers thinned out as the drivers tired and the rest areas and truck stops filled up. Dinner had been in a desert truck stop surrounded by sand and sage and flat country reaching out to the distant mountains to the north. Sleep had come after another two hours on the road in a rest area in western Oklahoma. As Jack wordlessly pulled off the interstate Amy knew it was time to quit for the night. Tomorrow would be the middle leg of this trip and probably the longest.

"Nice day's run", Jack mumbled as he returned from the bathroom pavilion with toothbrush in hand.

"Beautiful day to be out here", Amy replied. "No two days are ever alike are they? The colors are always different, the mountains are always changing. I'm so happy to be here with you, my Trucker Dude."

Jack looked at her for a long minute, considering what the wonder of her new experiences had brought to his own experience of the last few runs. Finally, he smiled and pulled the curtain separating the sleeper from the driving compartment closed.

"Always the same, always different. I'm real glad you're here too. Now get to sleep. Lots of ground to cover tomorrow."

Amy lie against her side of the cab reliving the day in her mind. Jack was quickly asleep, gently snoring, having ended his day and knowing what the next would bring. With his back turned away from her she could just see his outline next to her. He was not as big as Max or Alex, she thought, but he was strong in his own quiet way. She knew from hours spent alongside this little man that the thinning of his hair across the top of his forehead bothered him more than the flecks of gray at his temples. His features revealed his nature. Laugh lines surrounded his twinkling blue eyes. Even behind his sunglasses his eyes smiled as they streaked down the interstates together. Her full-of-wonder and questions, him the quiet tour guide.

Was it all routine for him, she wondered? Did he still see the little towns and the vastness that surrounded the stops along the way as she did? Had he asked her to join him to relieve boredom or to share the wonder of his life on the road?

Her admiration of his quiet confidence had grown each day, her own confidence growing as she learned from her road mate. Road Buddy, Trucker Dude,—strange names to describe their relationship to be sure. As she drifted off to sleep Amy wondered and then dreamt about their relationship, each getting something from the other; she knew their respect for each other was growing. But exactly what was it that they shared? She smiled sleepily, feeling comfortable and safe next to him and with him. She snuggled herself against his back as she drifted off.

Still feeling warm and safe as the sun rose hours later, Amy and Jack came gradually awake. Jack became aware of her arms around his ribs and of her warm softness snuggled into his back. Amy became aware of his reaction as they stretched together. It was still early. Not too early to get rolling but early enough to stay in bed for a little while longer. She reached for his face, kissed it slowly and then pulled him closer to her. She squinted into his laugh-lined eyes with that curious, questioning look, smiled, reached down and pulled her tee shirt off over her head.

His touch had been gentle at first, slowly tracing her outlines with his finger tips, slowly exploring her. She reacted to him with warmth and youthful energy. He stored away the memory of every part of her he touched in his own quiet way and finally finished with a power she hadn't expected and a groan she thought at first was some sort of pain as much as satisfaction. He held her for a long time with a tightness that made it hard for her to breathe. Silent and pressed together in the cab of his Peterbilt, they listened to the world come to life around them.

Typical for Jack, he said nothing when he returned from the truck stop washroom. He simply threw his bag into the back and completed his morning check of the rig. When finally in the driver's seat he just smiled and said again, "Lots of ground to cover", then added, "Dear." Amy just smiled and settled in for the day.

Three trips and half the Summer after that, Amy got to drive the big Peterbilt along a country lane paralleling the interstate and soon thereafter swaggered into the Lazy-R Truck Stop, flushed with the victory of driving on the interstate itself and piloting the big truck to a stop in front of the "other drivers".

"Watch the tach. Shift now. Double clutch, like I showed you." Jack's quiet instructions and reassuring smile when the big rig lurched to a little too much clutch built Amy's confidence.

"Ah hah, this is great. Let me stop and try it again, OK? I want to do it more smoothly. I know I can." Amy learned fast under Jack's patient tutelage

Facing the fears she had grown up with and testing the taboos she faced one by one, Amy's summer turned out to be all she had hoped for. Their trips back and forth across the country had kept her in a constant state of awe. She discovered and developed many of her own previously untested abilities. Quiet Jack, 'Mumbles' as he was known on the CB radio, gained his own small amount of fame among his peers on the East-West run for the young Seat Cover known as 'The Rookie' who traveled with him that summer. His calm, steady approach to all things, including their love-making, made discovering the danger he ran by allowing her to ride along in his company-mortgaged truck, letting her drive the monster that was his livelihood, and finally learning about his wife and family in their sedate neighborhood in Central LA, into an endless series of fears and fantasies conquered.

Los Angeles became their home base and the road became their own element. Amy, installed in a run down motel several miles from Jack's house, explored on her own with a self-assured confidence born of their time together. She walked along Venice Beach, exploring the shops and flirting with the body builders working out on the beach. She walked the long pier and talked to the old fishermen. Her confidence surged with each new experience and her manner showed it. No longer the shy bookworm, she saw herself as a traveler and a woman of the world, and this confidence made her appear more of what she showed herself as.

Sometimes, when Jack could get away, they would explore together. Even though he had lived in LA for years, Jack enjoyed showing his young friend the sites. They rode along the Pacific Coast highway in the smoking Maverick. They cruised the hills above the Malibu Colony with lots of other tourist types and stopped at the little clam shacks where the surfers hung out.

Amy was fascinated by the flashy people that populated this place and loved to ogle the big homes overlooking the beaches and sprinkled among the Hollywood hills.

Amy's summer seemed to stretch on forever. She hardly ever thought of who or what she had left behind.

Amy believed Jack's assertions that he had never spent a summer so engaged. She believed that this quiet man had always found it natural and appropriate to be true to his wife of twenty years until Amy had come along. She did not fully understand though what it was about her that had made him stray. He tried to explain that it was something to do with her fearlessness and her bold challenging of the world.

"You got to believe that I wasn't looking for you, young lady." he said, "You just got an attitude a lot of us got a need for."

Amy thought long and hard about this simple statement and its honesty only made her more driven to figure out this person she was becoming. She couldn't completely understand how someone with so many fears could seem fearless to others, but she was beginning to understand that her journey was something special.

Simply glorious, that's what life is, she thought as she ordered the special for herself and smiled back at Jack's shrugged shoulders and pushed back cap. "You sure did make yourself an entrance, young lady. It'll take me all year to live this down."

CHAPTER THIRTEEN

...After the Thrill

With the end of summer came the end of the adventure. A change in seasons brought a change in challenges. Amy had to admit to herself that the thrill of occasionally being allowed to pilot the big, phallic truck was beginning to wear thin. Soon the twin pressures from her folks to return to Baxter and Jack's wife to explain the subtle differences she had begun to notice in the sleeper after each trip began to mount. She also had to admit that the thrill of exploring the alien landscape of Los Angeles was beginning to pale with each successive return to that hot little hotel room and each furtive goodbye as Jack returned to his little bungalow on the tree shaded lot and his family.

Mom and Dad had been all too willing to buy the story about her "friend" Jackie she was spending the summer with. She sent them postcards from New Jersey regularly;—quick notes describing swimming and horseback riding with "Jackie" mailed from the post office near the eastern terminus of Jack's line. What they didn't know or want to know couldn't upset their little world.

Jack's wife was another story. Upon noticing the scents and touches of another woman, with the same quiet, calm determination that Amy had come to admire so much in Jack, she simply made sure a new picture of herself and the kids was hung in the sleeper when Jack picked up Amy for the next run. She insisted that it was his turn to take their little Stevie to the Cub Scouts meeting and just happened to be going through the family photo album when he returned home from an afternoon ride along the beach with Amy.

The euphoria of walking casually past the little bungalow that housed the Menand family soon began to wear. The yellow Maverick looked small and run down parked in the side yard. And knowing that the huge Peterbilt waited for both she and Jack in the company yard across town just made it all look even more depressing. Amy's energizing adventure became paled by the sight of the pain in Jack's eyes when she asked how his weekend had been.

She had her most recent exploration of Venice Beach to share. She had had the excitement of the nighttime crowd on the boardwalk to talk about. He had only a few words about the dying Maverick and his older boy Johnny's feet growing too fast. The guilt he felt didn't need to be said; it could be seen.

Jack was really only comfortable on the road. His wife, Sheila, was only happy in their little backyard and with her sons. They accepted each other and did not make unreasonable demands on one another, but they both shared the same determination. Jack waited for the next trip and the next load to bring him back to his open road and with it his freedom from the day to day details of life. Sheila waited until the guilt she knew would gradually build up in her man would bring him back to her.

Amy felt the guilt. Without many words, as was their custom now, she understood that her challenge and his infatuation were beginning to tarnish and fade as the realities of their situations crept inexorably into the picture. Jack was becoming increasingly embarrassed by the ribbing his fellow drivers gave him about his

'Ride-along Seat Cover', and Amy could tell. Although too much the quiet gentle man to tell her, she could tell that he was beginning to wonder if his summer of indiscretion had been such a good idea after all.

This too was part of Amy's learning curve that summer. Up to now her adventures had been about exploring and challenging herself. She pushed the limits to discover her limits. By doing the things she feared, she conquered them. Now she learned that these challenges to her self could affect others. She vowed not to hurt others with her adventures in the future. She decided that she didn't want to hurt nice people like her Jack.

Amy told her parents she would return in time for classes to start in the fall. She sent Alex a postcard from a truck stop in Arizona telling him when Jack would drop her off at school and asking him to please be there so she could show him 'her big Cabover Pete'.

THREE

FALL/WINTER

Later Still

CHAPTER FOURTEEN

...Change Comes With the Season

Conflicting emotions battled within Amy as she and Jack drove up the long hill to the campus. What had seemed so comfortable and had given her such thrills all summer suddenly seemed awkward and almost embarrassing. The big, white Peterbilt cab stuck out like the ultimate sore thumb amongst the station wagons and U-Haul trailers that the other students arrived in. She had been so proud all summer of the fears she had faced and the status she had achieved. Now, as she showed Jack her room and greeted her new roommate, she could feel one chapter closing and another beginning to open.

What challenge would there be for her here? She had done this before. She had experienced the college thing last year. She felt a sadness that she was returning to something she already knew and sadness that the simple times and quiet company of Jack's sleeper were ending.

She promised to await his phone calls from the road and vowed to meet him whenever his route could bring him reasonably close to Baxter. He promised to make his trips via upstate New York as frequently as he could. Although she could tell that he would miss her, she knew Baxter was not really near his usual interstate routes and that the little picture of the girl in the slightly too small 'Truckers Do It In The Road' tee-shirt and the cut-off jeans, looking up from the mid-summer roadside, squinting through her horned-rim glasses, a bundle of freckles and energy, would only grace the visor of his cab until he next returned to the little bungalow in L.A. and the Maverick with the bad head gasket.

She found herself looking only half-heartedly for Alex, not really wanting to show him the scene of all her summer adventures after all. She somehow knew he wouldn't have understood. She found herself wishing the big truck wasn't quite so noticeable as she said her good byes to Jack in the busy parking lot outside the residence hall. Their embrace was father/ daughterly and their kiss fleeting at best. The other students moving in all around them seemed too busy with their own good byes to notice the older man handing Amy a goodbye gift and for this, Amy and Jack were both grateful. They climbed into the cab for a little shelter. The Peterbilt hood ornament gift he had hidden under his seat shone in her hand and her eyes misted over as he gave it to her.

They talked in the cab for a little while and then she took one last look around the sleeper and jumped down. Jack inched it out of the lot, around the station wagons and the sedans. Amy waved as her summertime adventure rumbled down the big hill.

And she was right of course. Alex had seen the big, white truck parked just up the lot from his own car. He didn't go over although the curiosity regarding what his kooky friend and confidant had gotten herself into raged. The truck intimidated him and for the life of him he couldn't think what he might say to this Jack person Amy had written him about. He imagined a big, burly guy with huge shoulders and a leer in his eye. He imagined finding a hairy arm protectively hunched around his friend's slender form and a challenge just awaiting Alex's first false move.

The car he had been so eager to show off to Amy and his other friends seemed suddenly very small and insignificant in the same lot as the huge truck cab. He had been really proud of his first car and as eager to show it off as Amy had been eager to show off 'her' truck.

But who would be impressed, he thought now, with an eight-year-old sedan.

Who would be impressed, *she* thought now, with a small boned, balding trucker and his out of place tractor.

Alex made himself busy with moving in and greeting other friends and didn't find the time to get to Amy's room to see her until the ghostly and out-of-place presence in the parking lot was safely gone.

Alex didn't understand. But at least he tried to. Making him understand this thing that drove her was becoming, Amy realized, a new, small challenge in and of itself. So safe and afraid to deviate from his plans, Alex had gone back for the summer to the same job as he had had the previous summer. Alex was bronze colored from his summer at the Lakeside Marina. He had run the gas dock, helped launch and pull out the boats, worked a little in the Ship's Store and done some of the more simple work in the repair shop.

The marina had been a pleasant setting for his summer—just as planned. He had seen his latest girlfriend regularly and became what he thought was a more experienced and skilled lover. He had made enough spending money for another year at Baxter and saved enough on top of that, for his first car.

While comfortable with his progress, Alex began to wonder if his planned course was causing him to miss out on something. According to her occasional postcard, Amy had spent the summer doing things far beyond even Alex's imagination.

He had tried to throw himself into things the way his strange friend did. He wrote passionate letters to his current love, trying through his words to capture the romance he read into Amy's descriptions of her adventures. But it hadn't worked. Patty was nice. They had fun at the beach and on her Dad's boat and they made love around the pool in the cool summer evenings after the marina had closed. He was absolutely sincere in his expressions and passion but he was left feeling just a little incomplete. That little voice inside kept telling him that there was more.

Patty and he agreed to call each other sometime and he returned to Baxter itching to feel the passion he could write about and longing for that vitality that Amy's postcards brought vicariously to his planned, ordered life. If only he could find someone like Amy to inspire the passion he knew was within him, he thought.

CHAPTER FIFTEEN

Are You Crazy?

"Are you Crazy? Don't you *think* before risking your life?" When Alex and Amy finally got together to exchange notes and summer stories after dinner that first night back, his big brother attitude really came out. "Riding around the country in the hands of people you hardly knew. Living in a truck with a married man, breaking the law by driving one of those huge trucks without any proper training or licenses."

For all his admonishments and big brother scolding, Amy loved telling Alex all about her adventures as even *she* now called them. She was sure that deep down; he wished he could take the same reckless course.

Her affection grew for her big, conservative friend that term. Their relationship grew, not to the point of sleeping together, but certainly to a new kind of understanding for them both. As they both dug back into their books, they used each other to process their experiences. As they both thought and talked about their summers, their friendship grew. Although he kept seeing his "regular girl", there was something between them now that occasionally burst out in a kiss or look of longing between them that both could feel but neither was ready to consummate. Their need for each other was intertwined with their desire to understand each other and until it was untangled, they couldn't seem to take that next step. Amy needed Alex to put her experiences into perspective and Alex needed Amy to help him see beyond the ordered life he had built for himself.

Involved in school and student government, Alex filled up his days and evenings with productive pursuits. Involved in modern dance and the stage crew for the college theatre club, Amy continued to explore.

They saw each other occasionally. They made time for each other. Their relationship became one of catching up with each other's lives—bouncing ideas and achievements off each other for either reinforcement or criticism. Amy continued to seek the new and challenging and Alex, whether he realized it or not, continued to seek the passion that was missing from his life.

Alex kissed Amy good night after a particularly late night of telling stories and reliving some small measure of the excitement in the telling. He imagined himself quite the college man by now and felt proud of his relationship with the little Tomboy who was more than met the eye. He felt that his acceptance of her showed maturity and depth. He was sure that their ability to hug goodnight and kiss goodbye signified a friendship such as one was supposed to have as an adult. Walking down the long halls to his own room, climbing the stairs up to the men's floor, he told himself he was quite the college man—quite the accepting liberal.

He undressed for bed but found sleep elusive. He shifted from side to side in his not quite long enough, school issue bed and cursed quietly the covers that tangled around his legs. Sure, his plans were all working out. Sure he was succeeding according to schedule. Then what was missing? Why these late night arguments with himself about what was missing in his life? Was it Amy that left him with these doubts? Of course it was. Her approach, as much as he liked her, was wrong. Her unplanned, chaotic attack on life was sure to run her aground sooner or later. He needed to stop seeing her so much. He needed to separate from her a little. He drifted off to sleep.

Amy and Alex walked the beach together. Amy and Alex were entwined in each other's arms. He did love her after all, welling up with both passion and emotion. Her soft skin was warm to his touch. His body yearned for her. He felt complete with her.

Alex awoke. It was still too early to get up. His dreams were at once too passionate and too disturbing to allow sleep. Awake, he thought he should pull back from Amy. She confused him too much. Asleep, he wanted her, felt content and complete with her. Damn! Why did she always interfere with his plans?

What was this new spark he felt? Or perhaps it was an old spark. Once again he caught himself thinking of Amy as more than a friend. Was there something special in her kiss last night? Maybe she hadn't wasted her summer after all. He struggled to understand what it was that she brought to his life. He tried to analyze it as he would any other plan to be perfected. It wouldn't compute. He fought to make it fit. He drifted back to sleep.

'You know Amy, I really do love you', he stammered out.

'I know', she murmured in his dream.

Amy snuggled into her pillow a little more, three floors below. She realized that Alex had begun to truly love her. Amy could now see his love in a way she hadn't been able to before. This was not a game or a challenge to be experienced but a more long-term affection that would be there no matter where the rest of her life took her. Alex accepted her although he didn't always approve of her. His acceptance came without hurt. It didn't require a breaking down of her hard won confidence. He obviously felt attracted to her. The way he held her, when she allowed it, and the way he looked at her when she didn't, made that clear enough.

There was a new drive in his pursuit of her too. It was as if he wanted to escape his own ordered world through her one of practiced abandon. It was as if he could somehow, through loving her, feel some of the passion that facing her fears gave her.

His physical desire for her, when it occasionally emerged now seemed to suggest that a physical exchange between them could help him in some way to face the fears he could not even acknowledge within himself. She decided that to allow their relationship to become more than friendly would be a mistake. She would not allow his desire to find something within himself drive them to risk their friendship.

She slept peacefully.

CHAPTER SIXTEEN

Gracey and the Farm Boys ...

She ruled with an iron hand, a respect that no one dared challenge. No one, not even a stranger, would challenge Grace Browning. I remember seeing her throw out drunken salesmen too long on the road and two hundred and fifty pound farm boys too long in the field. So clear was the respect that everyone had for her, that failing to heed her command would mean having to deal with virtually all the customers on a given night as her back-up. She never, in my experience, had any trouble maintaining order in *her* bar.

Tiny, in her fifties or sixties maybe, hatchet-faced and slender, Gracey Browning was the barmaid at the Novelty Grill. And it wouldn't surprise me too much to find her still tending bar in some unique little place today.

The Novelty Lounge was just that—a novelty. In a college town crammed with bars that catered to the fall through spring invasion that doubled the population, the Novelty was never overcrowded. Where the other bars in Baxter held happy hours, sponsored softball teams and even hosted road rallies to bring in the college kids, the Novelty had no specials, no activities.

In fact, the Novelty almost never had college kids among its clientele.

Gracey allowed small groups of them in if one of them was celebrating a birthday or other special occasion but she would just not tolerate any of the loud antics and rude behavior that they were accustomed to across the street or down the alley from the Novelty's Main Street location.

The Novelty Lounge had one pool table, dark lights, Gracey the barmaid and *dancers*.

Mild by comparison with anything a bigger town could boast, the dancers at the Novelty were a leftover from the Go-Go days of the sixties. They did not gyrate naked in front of the customers or even topless. There was no lap dancing, touching of self or others or overtly sexual gyrations. Gracey would never allow that. The customers dared not exhibit the lewd, leering, stuffing bills into g-strings behavior I've seen in other towns. In fact, I'm not sure I ever saw even a hint of the prostitution that dancer equipped clubs fronted for in the city where I attended medical school. No, the customers in the Novelty quietly sipped their drinks and politely applauded or smiled their appreciation of Gracey's girls because that was the way Gracey wanted it.

Gracey would put a couple of quarters from the register in the juke-box and the disco beat would signal whichever of her girls was on that night that it was time to climb the stairs to the tiny stage behind Gracey's bar. The dancer would shed her cover-up and dance for the next twenty minutes—in proper bikini or negligee, of course.

I guess I took Amy there to show her that my life wasn't as straight-laced and as boring as she said it was. It had become important for me to show her that I could offer something that she wouldn't tire of right away. She was becoming more and more important to me by then and although I was still jealous of the at-ease abandon with which she attacked life, I felt comfortable enough with her that I wanted to count on her as someone who would be a part of my plan for a long time.

Anyway, I took Amy to the Novelty one Thursday night. I had gained Gracey's acceptance by baby sitting a few of my friends through her place on their birthdays. I guess I had shown enough cooperation and responsibility so that when I occasionally stopped in she would smile and nod her acceptance. I would say I was just stopping in to say hello and stay for a couple of beers while I watched her girls and learned that there were other kinds of women than the ones I was used to in my world.

I took Amy to the Novelty and damn if she didn't think it was a great thing. Here I was, taking a big risk—taking a girl I respected to the Novelty—and she took it all in stride. Of course, I should have known!

Even Gracey was impressed. Amy strode right in with that Tomboy walk of hers and stared more openly at the dancer than I was accustomed to doing. After Gracey's initial raised eyebrow, shot at me as we entered, she and Amy became fast friends.

Again, I should have known. Gracey didn't often get a lot of women that you'd like to talk to in her place (except her girls, of course) and Amy's smile and willingness to dive right into something new drew an immediate good rating from the Novelty's resident Queen Bee.

They talked as Gracey watched the bar, tended to her customers and as Kiki, a tall, flat chested black girl danced behind the bar. Kiki was a little too suggestive with some of her moves and the winks she was giving some of the farm boys did not meet with Gracey's usual standards. At the end of her twenty-minute set, Gracey frowned and said, "You can sit down Honey." and to Amy and I, whispered, "She won't last long."

I was already feeling left out with Amy and Gracey getting along so famously so imagine the sinking feeling I got when Amy asked, "How much do the dancers get paid?" and "Do they provide their own costumes?" and finally, "Would I have to audition or what?"

I damn near fell off my barstool! My Little Waif as a Dancer—

it was impossible! I had noticed that her summer on the road had made her body more lean and taut but she was much too plain! Who would watch? Another crazy stunt! My forehead bumped down on the bar top as Gracey said, "Sure thing, Honey, be here at four tomorrow and I'll introduce you to the owner", and then more quietly, casting a sidelong glance in Kiki's direction, "We'll see if we can't get rid of some of the bad eggs around here."

Oh no! She had no idea what she was saying! What had I done? My little Amy up there dancing? Well, I knew she wasn't *my* anything and at least I knew enough not to try to stop her.

Amy smiled at me, fairly bouncing up and down on the barstool with excitement. She gave me one of her most freckled, innocent looks. My forehead came down on the bar again and Gracey said, "Now stop that, Honey."

CHAPTER SEVENTEEN

... *The Good and the Very Bad*

She was good, this new one. She had possibilities and she was definitely different. Gracey smiled slightly as she set up for the evening. Fresh from the beauty parlor and prim in her white blouse and pink slacks, she allowed herself a little reflection.

Wendy was older but was the best dancer. She was smart too. *Wendy's Dance Studio* upstairs would be her ticket out of this life when she was too old to gyrate up on that stage. Even now, she was obviously a little older than the other girls, but nobody seemed to mind when she danced. Smooth and cultured and athletic, she sprinkled just enough of the modern dance she taught her daughter's little friends upstairs to give the impression that there was something smoldering within when she peeked out from behind her long black tresses.

Dawn was more exotic. Her dark coloring and low-hipped swinging suggested a Polynesian flavor that went over well in the dark room. Although really Italian, her big-breasted hula and long straight black hair had the customers thinking Hawaii on even the coldest nights.

Betty was just off the farm. Blond and fresh-faced, all high cheekbones and pigtails, she was seeking a big break which was not likely to come dancing at the Novelty. Broadway producers didn't often wander upstate looking for cute blondes to make into stars but if it made her happy to wish, who could deny her those dreams?

Amy was different though. At least Gracey thought so. First of all she was a college student and they almost never wanted to join her girls. Dancers came from all walks on their way to Gracey's bar but only once before had one come from the college on the hill.

Gracey knew and understood her place in the scheme of things and it had little to do with the kids from the college. She and her girls served Baxter in other ways. Mr. Grant, the owner, was served by the steady cash flow from a building long paid off and by the fact that Gracey needed little help supervision or checking-on to run the Novelty. Grant puffed in daily to stock the refrigerated cases behind the bar for Gracey and to count the previous night's receipts. He visited Wendy upstairs at her studio occasionally and bestowed upon her the title of Head Dancer, but other than that, he left the running of his little gold mine to Gracey.

The 'betters' of Baxter were served by the Novelty because they had something they could turn their noses up at as they rushed past on the sidewalks outside.

Those traveling through and those escaping the wife for a few hours had a place to go and dream without it getting all around town. In fact, Gracey guessed even the college was served by the spice her placed added to an otherwise typical college downtown.

Different, a little spicy, a little scandalous but hers was definitely not really a bad place. Good clean fun, and at her age that was important. Thirty years as a Bartender and she could still hold her head up high in church on Sundays. Scoff if you want you 'betters' Gracey knew that her place was not really bad for anyone.

At first Amy had been very tentative. It was funny how she had practically hired herself and how she had seemed so eager to jump into this new thing and then had had so much trouble getting started. She seemed so innocent on the one hand yet so willing to jump in on the other. Gracey had come to almost admire this one over the past few weeks.

Amy was a strange mix of innocence, vitality and yes, a little fear as well. Look at how timid she had been those first few nights on the stage behind her bar.

Gracey was good at not showing it but she saw everything that happened in her place.

Amy's first get-up was just a bathing suit. As Bikinis went it wasn't even that skimpy and her steps were routine at best. Gracey wasn't all that sure that she'd work out but she had wanted to get rid of Kiki. Too much flirting out of that one and too much flashing of her little breasts at the customers when she thought Gracey wasn't looking. But this Amy was a trouper. She had a lot of determination. She came in with that tall boy even when she wasn't working and watched the other girls. She talked to Wendy about costumes and where to shop and how to stitch on a fringe or how to hike up the side of her bikini bottom. Pretty soon her costumes got a little more imaginative and she started picking up steps from the other girls. A little fringe along her bust line and a little twist to her swaying hip and darn if she didn't develop a following of sorts.

The farm boys liked her clean, freckled exterior and out-of-towners liked her too. Gracey was quietly disdainful of them for it—fantasizing about a girl who could easily be their own daughter in most cases but as long as they maintained the respect she demanded in her place, she guessed it couldn't do too much harm. It was just another service provided by the Novelty Lounge.

Amy's big friend seemed OK too. At first he'd be in every night she worked. The tall kid with what was probably his first mustache would sit at the end of the bar trying to look as big as and possessive as possible. Once or twice Gracey had to tell him not to glare so at the other customers when they gawked at Amy or made admiring comments. A couple of times there were even a few cross words between the Amy and her escort.

Alexander (she was pretty sure that was his name) had at first stood firm, insisting that Amy needed someone to keep an eye on things—almost implying that she couldn't do so herself. He hinted that left to her own devices, Amy couldn't be trusted to keep from doing something crazy.

Gracey had started to say that he needed to relax a little and let her take care of things in her place and then Amy had really lit into him. 'Who was he, to try to protect her? Didn't he understand her yet? Watch it or she'd have Gracey kick him out'.

Well that deflated him soon enough and although he still came around some nights, there seemed to be a wall now between these two kids who had been friends (and maybe a little more than friends). Alex stopped coming in every night that Amy worked. Amy seemed to have moved on. She became more and more comfortable with the lace and the frills and the moves. She still maintained that somewhat innocent air about her but there was now mischief in those eyes—as if she was looking for something new to conquer.

And recently now, Gracey had begun to wish that the tall kid would come back and sit at the end of the bar more often.

CHAPTER EIGHTEEN

... For Those Too Stupid

Steven Michaels was a Parole Officer. Parole he figured was for those dirt bags too stupid to survive in society without a baby sitter. It was a crappy job but someone had to do it. He didn't subscribe to any bull shit about helping these losers blend back into society. The vast majority were just that—losers. All you could do was shake 'em down and keep 'em scared.

Actually, the pay was OK. The fear he could inspire was great. The connections didn't hurt either. All the free booze, pot or women he could want were usually within easy reach and who was going to rat on him—the dirt bags? He even made a little scratch on the side once in a while working as the "middleman" for friends who needed to score.

In his capacity as official baby sitter to the lowlifes of Treadwell County he made it his business to check the Novelty Lounge in Baxter on a regular basis. It was always good ammunition for a little scare to catch one of his parolees in the place and in spite of the old bag behind the bar, there was usually a nice piece of ass to look at.

Once in a while you could even get a little lucky. That black bitch, Kiki, had been so hot for him a couple of months ago, he thought she would break his tool right off. Maybe she thought he could put in a good word for her with Gracey but the old bitch had fired her anyway. Last he had seen that hot little number, she had been turning tricks down at the county fair in Ashton. She had been hot, that's for sure, but for now he could wait for another piece to come his way. Kiki would turn up on his list of parolees or probationers before long—unless he missed his guess.

Friday had been slow. He checked-up on Sloan, out at the golf course and had a couple of beers for lunch at the bar out there. He checked-up on a couple of broom pushers out at the electronics plant and then did some paperwork at the office.

On the way home to his place on Culver Street, he had decided to stop at the Novelty to see who Gracey had gotten to replace Kiki. He was disappointed when it was just that new college kid he'd heard about and not someone who would be an easy shot. He smiled at Gracey as he sauntered in and she glared back disapprovingly.

He sat down just to piss her off. What the hell, he had the right to be there no matter what she thought of him. After all, he knew her boss, and Bill Grant would be more than happy to keep him happy. Grant needed no close scrutiny of his relationship with that Wendy Wilson bitch and Michaels could at least threaten that scrutiny if he wanted to.

He sat at the bar and grumbled an order for a beer and watched the college kid. Smooth skin. Not a junky or user that he could tell. Nice boobs. A little thick around the thighs for his tastes though. Michaels liked to feel bones when doing a chick. Her hair was up in a way that kinda looked sophisticated but the little freckled nose contrasted in a way that made her look like a kid trying to play grown-up.

He smiled at her with his best invitation smile and smoothed his thinning hair forward across his brow. He wondered if the girl could see how thin it was getting from up on the stage.

He was surprised when she smiled back. As she gyrated and swung to the music in the almost empty room she gazed dreamily at him with a look that was hard to figure. He thought he saw fear. He was sure he saw defiance or challenge and there was a gleam of excitement deep in those big browns almost like a jittery parolee on something. It was funny but that dreamy look made him feel a little weird—like prey. He was used to inspiring nervousness in a parolee he had something on but it was a little unsettling to be looked at like a target himself—almost like he was an experiment and the college kid was the scientist inspecting the raw material under her microscope.

Gracey, that old bat, stepped in between them to bring his beer, stood there until he put some money on the bar and then, as she turned away without a word, shook her head in the negative at the kid in a way that was subtle but impossible to miss. Gracey did not approve.

CHAPTER NINETEEN

... Who's in Control Here Anyway?

When he awoke Sunday morning he heard her on the phone in the kitchen. She was OK she was telling someone he supposed was a roommate or something. She said something about exploring 'the darker side of Baxter'. He didn't think that sounded too good.

The roommate or whoever, was to tell someone named Alex when he came by that she had to rush home unexpectedly for the weekend.

Michaels felt strange. It had been a weird night with this college kid—Amy, he had found out. She had been excited, almost giggly, and had treated him almost like a prize to be hoarded.

This, he was not used to. And she was still here, her yellow rag top convertible still in the driveway outside his window. She had made love strange too. She wasn't drunk or stoned. She didn't just lie there or go off into her own private world like some did. She had paid attention to it all, had seemed to analyze it all and that had somehow turned him on in a big way. He had decided to pound her without mercy to show her who was boss and had cum early when she had wiggled under him with glee.

He wondered again now, as she ran back into the bedroom, oversized tee-shirt from his laundry pile looking like something from a slumber party and jumped onto the bed, who was in charge here anyway. She looked even younger without the makeup that she had had on last night. Her eyes were big with excitement. Her face freshly washed.

"Gonna cook me breakfast, Michaels?" she asked the cigarette smelly man with the stale morning breath. "Want to go for a convertible ride? It's not too cold for you, is it?"

The kid seemed to be enjoying her self but Michaels wasn't sure this had been such a great idea. He almost felt guilty. It seemed like someone was being taken advantage of here—he just wasn't sure if it was him or her.

He had things to do. He had a card game with Jimmy Pizzola and the guys tonight. Yet Amy seemed in no hurry to get back to the college on the hill. She showed no concern regarding her predicament. It was as if she regularly went home with thirty-seven year old men she didn't know.

"OK, OK," he grumbled, why don't you come back later? We'll grill up something out back."

Maybe he had misjudged her. Maybe the innocent look was just a lot of crap. With this thought the night before began to feel dirty. But no, there was that look of fear and questioning intermingled in her eye again. Michaels was too good a judge of character. This was just as out of character for her as it was S.O.P. for him. What the hell, he thought. He rolled over on top of her again.

CHAPTER TWENTY

...*Surrounded By the Children*

Revolting. Disgusting. He was an obviously bad man no matter what his badge said. Michaels was an older person with a bad smell and a worse smelling apartment. The seamier side of town indeed. She asked him about his work and about the people he knew and dealt with.

As she met the other bad people he knew, played cards with, sold dope for and drank with, she could clearly see the danger and ugliness of this part of Baxter and the world she had now discovered. It was terrifying, and wasn't that just the point? It was so terrifying that it gave her an amazing new clarity. Who needed drugs when the thrill of hanging out with these bad people and of sleeping with one of the powerful bad people in this dangerous, scary underbelly of her college town gave her an ability to experience every detail as if it was under a microscope?

Amy tried to explain it to Alex in the weeks that followed. "Oh come on Pal, I can take care of myself. I hitched across the whole damn country didn't I?"

She tried to explain it to Gracey. "It's just research. I won't get involved in anything that could hurt me. If I can figure out what makes people like Steve Michaels tick, maybe I'll be able to really learn something."

She tried to explain to herself that she was certainly getting a better education this way than had she been sitting in a classroom up on that hill. School, College, that once important chance to break away from her fears and doubts was now becoming little more than a chore. It was, she felt, something holding her back from her education rather than the source of that education.

It was time to move out of the dorms and into town where she could continue to attend Baxter but not be surrounded by children. She moved out of the residence halls and into an old house on Park Street. It was just up from the old rail depot, not really in the part of town that the other college kids lived in. It was walking distance from the Mill Street bars that she would occasionally still frequent with Alex or her girlfriends. It was three blocks from Steve's and best of all, it was private. No roommate to explain to. She had the freedom to come and go as she wanted, be a part of the bar scene or not, stay with Steve or not. She became a part of Baxter rather than merely a visitor.

It was also time to quit 'Show and Tell' for the Farm boys. She loved Gracey but it was time to move on. She loved Alex but she couldn't let him hold her back. She'd explain it to them and surely they'd have to understand. Any less terrifying choice just wouldn't make it anymore. She was addicted to the thrill now.

FOUR

SUMMER TIME

Quite a While Later

CHAPTER TWENTY-ONE

...Like I Belong

It's really beautiful here. Dozens of boats, large and small, dot the harbor. They're mostly pleasure boats this time of year, mostly small day sailors and cabin cruisers.

I can't help feeling that I was meant to live in a place like this. No, I don't necessarily mean Kent, Rhode Island. Not necessarily an old Caretaker's cottage, overlooking this little bay harbor. Certainly not in a place where the wind whips up the bay in the winter and where it rains all through the spring and the fog rolls in more often than not the rest of the year. No, this isn't what I had always imagined for myself. Except in summer—that's when I feel like I belong here.

Summer in New England—the air dries out and the land turns green. The sun beats against the dark red storm shutters on the house and your soul warms up a little. In summer you don't feel as sorry for the solitary Quahoggers, racing across the bay in their open skiffs to where they know the great clams rest.

In winter you have to feel for them as they huddle down behind their little doghouse shelters in their otherwise open boats. In summer you can envy them their good, hard, difficult work and lives. They look as if they might almost have time to enjoy the warmth of the sun and cool of the bay.

My cottage looks a little weather beaten, but I've come to accept that as a true indication of its New England authenticity. The gray shingles were of course brown years ago, with the look of new wood, but they have now earned the right to mellow to that watery gray that pervades these regions. Their years facing little Kent harbor have matured them, just as I feel today, the years have matured me.

The house is small, but not uncomfortably so. Bachelors such as I don't cart around all that much useless junk anyway.

My cottage is known to the locals as The Foreman's House. The Foreman, a person of evidently considerable stature and status with the locals was the one who supervised the stable boys, the gardeners and the numerous other regular and part-time employees of the Richmond family.

Being entrusted with the running of the one truly great estate in Kent gave this individual great powers of patronage. Whenever an addition needed to be put on to the big house on the point or the plumbing wore out or the roof needed mending, Almeida Construction or Silva Excavating or Souza & Sons Plumbers would suddenly appear as the local contractor of merit. Never mind that a relative of the Foreman always owned the company. That was only to be expected. Those in the town who were not related to the Foreman never openly resented his family's ascendancy. They simply waited their turn or quietly planned to marry a daughter or a son into the family with the proper connections.

One of the perks that went along with the Foreman's job was this cottage—or so I'm told. It's actually across the road from the main property, 'let's not get silly, it was OK to hire the Portuguese to work for you, but must they also live on the same property'?

The cottage was built by the Richmonds, repaired and maintained out of the Richmond's household budget and since the Richmonds never visited it after its construction for their first Foreman, it was maintained in the finest of condition by the Foreman and his many relatives.

The Richmonds—those still left—no longer live on the estate proper but in a tastefully expensive home overlooking the bay further out toward the bridge and the College. After the mill the first Richmond built was used to make millions during the two world wars (I think that one was Issac Richmond), and after that same, now aged mill was closed after the last big war, those left with the family name seemed content to live off those millions generating millions and moved into a more comfortable, newer home in what was now a better section of town.

My cottage remains a footnote to all that Richmond history. The main estate is now a park. The big house has long since surrendered to the weather and rot. My cottage, along with most of the other public lands in Kent and along with the land the College was built on, was all donated to the town or the state years ago, to provide much needed tax breaks for the remaining Richmonds.

And now I live in the Foreman's cottage. It is a place in which I usually feel very comfortable. I look across my yard to the sea wall and the harbor, across the harbor to the old mill buildings and the rest of the village that has stood here, at the edge of the water, since before another war—the Revolutionary. It usually feels right—according to plan.

As Staff MD for Kent-Richmond College, the cottage is mine for as long as I stay. This works out well for me and for KRC. I get to live in a much sought after, waterfront location and they get to pay me considerably less than I'm worth by justifying the house as a part of my salary and remuneration. My needs are relatively simple. A roof and enough of a salary to keep me out of trouble. The waterfront cottage is just the kind of bonus careful planning brings.

After all, isn't this exactly what I've planned for all these years? Isn't all this according to plan? Baxter College led to Albany Medical School, internships and residencies in Boston, and finally, here I am—just as planned. A college Medical Doctor treating basic and minor ailments, looking mostly at minor student complaints and living the good life. This is the life I've always wanted. I'm near the water, near a good, public golf course and financially secure. It's comfortable and just another step on the ladder. Soon will come the country club and private practice. Then too, the larger home overlooking the water, a couple of afternoons of golf each week and a wife and two point three children waiting at home.

Granted, my first attempt at marriage didn't work out exactly as planned but I blame that failure on med. school and the strains of residency. Julie was a good wife and partner and I really did love her, but after a couple of years, we were living as strangers. She said that we had become bored.

It was probably a mistake to get married right after undergraduate school, but even though it wasn't part of the plan, it seemed the logical thing to do at the time. Julie and I had been together for well over a year. My prospects were good. I had already started med. school. She pointed out that two were supposed to be able to live more cheaply than one...

I guess she just got tired of waiting for the good life to arrive. She wanted more excitement in her life. Well, I suppose she's got that now. Last I heard she was living with some musician in Greenwich Village.

It nearly killed me that she would prefer such an uncertain life to what we had planned. There would be no assurances, I told her. There'd be no way of knowing that you will be able to survive year to year.

"You bore me," she had said, and I had to agree that it had all become routine for us.

I got over it though. It just took me a while to get back on track...to get the plan back in order.

I've always been able to do that. That's one of my strengths. Oh, I might get distracted or a little confused now and then when the unexpected happens, but give me a little time and I'm back on an even keel.

That's why I'm a good doctor. I can look at a patient and analyze symptoms and circumstances until the correct diagnosis becomes apparent. Not much disrupts me. If a patient doesn't respond to a treatment right away, I don't let it throw me. I just look at the next most logical answer. My professors and supervisors in training were always impressed with my resolve, my methodical approach and my ability to handle the unexpected.

So what's wrong with me today? Why am I suddenly so introspective that I can't do too much else but reflect on the past? I often sit here on my wide, old porch and watch the boats glide by. What is there about today that causes me to be filled with longing for something else?

All right, let's analyze it. What's happened in the past few days that would have bothered me into this condition? Work has been normal. We've dealt with the usual flu and menstrual cramps. I've been a party to the usual politics and budget arguments that seem to come so consistently with a small school.

Jenny said just the other day, that the politics I grouse about all the time are just one more experience to be savored, just one more aspect of life to delight in, learn from and to draw energy from. Doesn't she understand how draining all this petty nonsense can be? What does she mean 'draw energy from the challenges'?

She is such a bundle of energy, that one. She's so sure of herself at only twenty. She seems willing and eager to run the whole infirmary office if I'd let her. She's quite a bargain for her hourly work-study wages. Boy does she have spunk. All blond hair and bubbling enthusiasm, she has more than enough energy to attack the world. She's reminiscent of Amy.

Gosh, I haven't thought about Amy in a long, long while. I wonder where she is now, or if she has even survived all her adventures. She had the same desire to attack the world that Jenny the work-study student has. She tried to squeeze every bit of

103

experience from life that she could before her time was up here. I tried to protect her when we first met, tried to understand her after we became friends, became frustrated as hell by her outlook as we struggled to become more than that. I gave up too soon, I guess. I guess I didn't analyze her as well as I should have.

The tangents she went off on though, the windmills she chased down. Oh, to have had her courage—or foolhardiness.

I wonder if I ever really loved Amy or whether I was just infatuated with her approach to life? I wonder if she ever knew what I felt. She always seemed to have that same inner wisdom I now see in Jenny, as if she could see right through to the heart of me. As if she could see past all the grousing and posturing—to what was really important.

I distinctly remember trying to explain to her how I felt. We were sitting on the porch of that run down duplex apartment she was renting our junior year at Baxter. She was telling me about her latest conquest. It was something about a parole officer that played cards and dealt drugs on the side. She was so excited about the world she was discovering that she couldn't really hear my awkward attempts to profess my love.

I don't know why it seemed so important to tell her that I thought I loved her. Perhaps I was looking to share her confidence. Perhaps I was just desperate for something unplanned and unexpected. I was sure looking for something.

If I'd been more accepting of her, there's no telling where I'd be today. There's no telling what adventure she would have dragged me off on. Who knows if I would have ever attained my career goals, my plans? Dr. William Alexander Clark—it sounds as distinguished as it makes me feel. Yet, Amy ... where was she the last time I heard from her?

I guess it was pretty soon after I arrived here in Kent. I was blindly infatuated with Chris that summer. I was fresh from divorce, astounded at my good fortune to have landed this plum assignment for myself and Amy's short, disjointed (pleading?)

letter reached me when I was too wrapped up in Chrissy's dark Portuguese complexion, voluptuous curves and playfully willing nature to pay much attention to what Amy's words from my past were trying to say to me.

'I'm sitting here smoking another cigarette and there's a card game going on in my living room,' it began. 'These people are so purposeless sometimes. They waste their life away doing drugs and killing time. I'm seeing the local army recruiter, a Major. He spends all his days talking young men into the slavery that is our army. I'm sick of it. I'm not a part of the campus anymore and I don't really feel a part of any of this scene either. I actually got some college credit for all this, a Sociology experiment I sold Dr. Goodman on. This experiment is a little out of control lately.'

I remember wondering what the letter was all about but I never wrote back, scared of what the answers would have been to all my questions.

CHAPTER TWENTY-TWO

All This and Passion Too...

Amy rolled over toward the large, dark, sleepy man on her left and murmured; "I want to tell you how complete you make me feel". She pushed her short hair back from her face and continued, "You add balance to my life. You make me truly happy". She stretched luxuriously on the hilltop grass, arched her back, and rubbed her breasts along the man's side. In her white cotton sweater and tan shorts she looked the picture of health. She looked around at the German countryside, glanced mischievously over at her man's muscled arms and the slight sheen of sweat beading up on his brow and warmed to her topic.

"Today is an exceptional day," she went on as he lay next to her feigning disinterest. "It's a day that would make any woman happy. The sky has been bluer than blue all day, the air so clean, it's crisp. The greens of the hills and fields we can see from here are absolutely vivid. I can see so many different greens, so many variations on the same theme. I'm not sure I've ever seen green so beautiful. The other colors are beautiful too, of course. Little purple flowers that my mother would have known the name of and tiny black-eyed, yellow-petal Susans or whatever they are. The colors and the clarity of the day make it all more beautiful than reality should be allowed to be. There's no humidity like back home. There's no heat like down south—just crisp, clean air. Each tree seems almost close enough to touch. Each leaf, individually defined, is distinguishable as it gently turns its underside to catch its share the light afternoon breeze. This is the kind of beautiful day you dream but seldom experience".

"It is truly an exceptional day; truly, a happy time in my life", sitting up and crossing her legs, Indian style, "A girl can't ask for too much more out of life. It's as if the whole world has come to a stop; a final, long-earned stop after a hectic, busy, wild ride. And I finally feel like I can rest along with this busy world. Finally, I feel that I've found what I've always looked for".

"And a big part of that is you, my love". She brushed her hand across his cheek and he smiled dreamily.

"My job is great. It challenges me. It feeds my need for the new and different. It keeps me from getting bored. Who would have thought that the military could turn out to be the way of life for me"?

She untangled her legs and straddled the now smiling man, knees along side of his broad chest, bending down to lovingly harass him face to face. "A long time ago, I set out to challenge my fears and grow by doing what I feared most. Now I finally find myself rewarded by doing and performing at the edge of my own personal envelope. Like those Fighter Jocks we ran into in Cologne I am stretched daily to do all that I am able. Finally, I am challenged to use my brain, to put out for something important. Finally, I am valued for what I can do".

He turned his face away, mocking her, but she continued. "It may not seem that what I do is very glamorous, but I know things that few people know. I understand what countries do to keep ahead, even when the war isn't officially declared. Whether it's interpreting data from listening posts along with you, or debriefing refugees, I see what countries do to each other. I see what politics and power can do to innocent people".

"I've come a long way from hitchhiking across the good old U. S. It's been a long time since I danced at the Novelty".

"Not that long, my love. You are still beautiful enough to dance," the man mumbled sleepily.

"Thank you, I think I could still do it too," she said, quickly kissing him on the mouth before going on. "I'm certainly in better shape these days".

"What a strange journey it's been from my shy school girl days in Albany to this beautiful, quiet hillside with you here in Germany. Who would have thought that the trouble I got myself into in Baxter could have turned out so good? I really joined the Army to confront the crap I saw the local recruiters getting away with, you know. How small their little drug deals and kickbacks and double deals seem now. The knowledge we have, the power of what we know, that's the real rush. It isn't the danger I love, it's the knowledge".

"Fulfillment at last. All these years searching, daring, pushing the limits of good sense and I find contentment in using my brain, enjoying a simple summer day and your love".

"You love me without judgement, Dwayne." Staring intensely into his eyes now, him still feigning disinterest, "you accept me for what and who I am. There's no need to defend myself or my choices, no need to be afraid. You don't want to change me. I can tell you who I am and where I've been and what I've done and know that it will be OK with you. I've told you things about myself that I've told nobody else. It all comes out so easy, when I talk to you. I don't need false pride or false modesty. I can tell you and know that you won't judge or condemn. I can tell you my innermost thoughts and in the telling, understand them better myself".

"You have brought me peace, my love. You have brought me, through the power of your wisdom and gentle love, to myself. I have learned, finally, to love and be content, and for that I will always be grateful". She kissed him again, harder.

"I can't imagine being without you. I know you don't want to talk about this, but I want to be your wife more than anything in this world. I want to be your partner in all things. I don't care what the Army says about the difference in our ranks and I certainly don't care about any other differences that might slow down people that care about such things. You are beautiful to me and those who can't see beyond your skin color or mine can just go to hell. I want to be with you and I want us to be bonded together forever". She brushed her lips gently along the stubble of his cheek.

"All that I have and all that I've become—this makes me happy. I feel like I've been looking for this time with you all my life. I don't want it ever to end".

"And on top of it all, I have passion too. I've never felt the kind of passion we have with any other man. With nobody else, have I felt that it was so right. I have no reservations. I make no compromises. There is no settling. There is electricity between us. A passion felt and almost touchable. An understanding and an equality in our desire and love for one another. Our passion is that special, once in a lifetime thing that they make those movies you hate so much about".

"I am a grateful girl today," smiling into his eyes, "grateful that we have all this beauty around us and that we have passion too. I am grateful that I have all that I have found in this life and you too, my love".

"Now make love to me again before we have to go back to the base".

CHAPTER TWENTY-THREE

Are You Just A Mid Life Crisis?

'Darcy my dear, are you just a mid-life crisis?' Alex stared at the ceiling and shifted uncomfortably. He gazed unhappily out the window at the evening lights of Kent across his lawn and the little bay. He rolled his back toward the softly snoring woman next to him in his bed. 'God help me,' he thought, 'you sure seem like it tonight. Look how crazy this has all gotten. You, sleeping here beside me, me thinking guilty, self-deprecating thoughts. I wish I could wake you up and tell you all these things. But you wouldn't understand. All full of love, to you this isn't a game at all.'

'I think, in this early evening clarity that haunts me, that I was probably more bored with my life than attracted to you. You seemed so upbeat and full of energy, so young and fresh. Even newer to the College than I was, you are rapidly making a name for yourself as a 'doer'—a person with a future. You are really too young for me—and much too married.'

Alex rolled back toward the sleeping woman but couldn't bring himself to touch her. He continued his silent harangue of himself.

'I feel most guilty when I think of your husband. He seems such a good chap. He understands your crazy work hours and really doesn't question when you come home late. You tell me that he works hard and that he supports your graduate school classes with extra shifts. He really doesn't deserve where this has to ultimately go.'

'I guess it was an ego thing. I was so proud of my new boat that I bragged to everyone who would listen to me. Wanting to learn to sail was just a natural thing for someone as inquisitive as you. I should have known better. Just you and I on the boat, on the bay, your husband at work; it was a mistake just waiting to happen. Yeah, you learned to sail all right.' Alex's fist bunched on the sheet beside him.

'And now look at us—the school doctor and the school's director of housing. They both love to sail. They spend lots of time together after work. Her husband Eddie doesn't mind. He's always busy working, and how else could she afford sailing lessons?'

'And we sneak off to our secret rendezvous when it's too rough to sail. Or we linger just a little too long putting the boat to bed after an afternoon on the bay. The sex is good, at least for me. And you certainly don't seem to mind. You profess your love so easily. You give yourself so willingly. And I wake up feeling guilty.'

'If you are just a mid-life crisis, and I guess that by thinking about it this way, I'm confirming that you are, then why am I letting it continue?' Alex un-bunched his hand and rubbed his bearded chin. 'I know that you'll be hurt when it's over. I know poor Eddie will be crushed if it all comes out. There's no telling what it could mean to your job and my career.'

'I'm not supposed to be this kind of guy,' now rubbing his brow. 'I'm the moral one. I'm the one who takes the safe track. Why do I keep letting myself get off track so badly? What am I lacking that drives me to the edge of what I should be? What am I afraid of—being too normal? All I've ever wanted to be was a normal guy. I had plans. I had a nice comfortable envelope. Why can't I be happy with what I have? What am I lacking?'

'Why do I need a mid-life fling? That's something people who are bored or dissatisfied get involved with. Why do I have this compulsion to push beyond the safe and secure? What am I afraid of?'

'Life is a funny thing, I guess. It isn't enough to have a plan. You also have to have fire. Maybe I've always been afraid of the fire. I've always been so safe in my plans and goals that I haven't allowed myself to experience the spice in life. Maybe, dear Darcy, you are an expression of my need for that fire. Maybe suppressing that need for so long is what keeps driving me to situations like this one—detours from the plan, risks I know better than to take.'

'Maybe you represent the fire that makes me complete.' Alex quietly slipped out of the bed, slipped on his boxers and wandered the quiet cottage.

FIVE

ALMOST TOO LATE

CHAPTER TWENTY-FOUR

Dear Alex...

Hi, Old Buddy,

I hope this letter finds you. I tracked you to Boston through Albany Med. and they sent me on to Kent-Richmond. I hope you're happy and settled. I talked to my old roommate Debbie a couple of months ago (three kids and big as a house—living on Long Island and married to a Real Estate genius of some kind). She said that she heard that it didn't work out for you and Julie. Sorry. Sometimes life's a real bitch.

I guess you wouldn't have heard that I was married for a while too! He was the best guy in the world! He was named Dwayne Rogers and we met in Germany. We were both stationed over here. He was in intelligence (an officer) and I was still a grunt because of that whole mess I got into with that recruiter guy I was living with after college (Major Dixon, remember?). Dwayne was the most beautiful man you've ever seen and he loved me more than anything. I was so in love that I could think of nothing else but being with him. I think I was finally happy Alex.

We were married two months when he was killed in a stupid, pointless, needless accident. I'll tell you all about it someday.

After I lost him, the Army had to kind of take care of me for a while. I wasn't good for much. I wanted to call you but I couldn't get it together enough to be able to find you. I knew that old Doctor Clark would listen to his worn out friend.

Anyway, I've signed up for Air Traffic Controller's school back in the states. What do you think of that? Your "Little Waif" handling a radar screen?

I'd really like to see you if I get enough leave time between when they ship me back and school starts. I need to hear about your plans and successes and failures (come on, I know there must be one or two). I need to know someone still cares.

I'll call you when I get back to the states.

Your always friend,

Amy

Alex drifted back to a warm spring day, talking to Amy about her fears, about facing them and building her confidence. She spoke about the 'adventures' she had been on. They had sounded more like problems to Alex. She was wasting herself he thought. Angry at her for choosing the life she had, angry at himself for not being able to make her see the folly of her adventures he cut himself off from the emotions he felt for her.

It had been a long time since he had thought about Amy. Now he began to wonder about her again and perhaps more importantly, about himself. Finally, he began to be able to articulate in his own mind the jumbled up emotions he had tried to express to her on that porch in Baxter so long ago. What he needed to feel fulfilled, was her quest for the fire in life—her ability to stretch herself into the riskier areas of life—to challenge the things she feared in life. He needed that part of her which was most alien to him to make himself feel whole. He needed the risk-taking he had always been afraid of and driven nonetheless toward. He needed to stop hiding his fear in his plans and safe course.

But Amy wasn't complete either. Amy described herself as worn out. It was obvious that her fearless appearing course had taken its toll.

Perhaps he had been trying to realize, all those years ago, that what they both needed was each other. She needing the foundation he could provide, he needing the fire she sought.

How stupid it was of him to realize it all now. Approaching middle age, locked into a life with only borrowed thrills, past the point of changing the course of his life, he realized now what had been special about Amy. His time connected to her was that one time in life when what you needed was equal to what you had to give. He had blown it and it had taken him almost fifteen years to realize it.

Alex wondered if he would ever get another chance to be made whole.

Chapter Twenty-Five

Dear Friends and Lovers...

Friday evening Dr. Clark slumped on his porch swing. He stared out at the water and his twenty-four footer gently swinging at her anchor chain a few yards out into the little bay. Motionless, he sat and thought and waited. Alex waited for something to help him out of the funk he found himself in. The sun slowly set behind the house and the lights of the village began to twinkle on the water. Alex waited and thought and waited and brewed.

Finally he felt it fall into place. He knew what he must do. He made an inner commitment to himself. He tingled with fear yet felt cleansed by the decision—and alive again.

Alex sat down at his computer on Tuesday morning at 7:00 am. He looked across the room at the big old mirror that had come from his Grandmother's house. In it he saw gray in the mustache he had been so proud of once upon a time. He turned his head to look at the gray beginning to come in at the temples as well and wondered briefly if it was too late. He self-consciously checked the lines around his eyes as the word processor warmed up and wondered how long it would be before his mother's family pattern caused a bald spot to appear. Not really dressed for work in spite of an 8:30 am appointment, he began to write.

Afraid of Me

My Dear Dr. Dempsey,

I regret to inform you, at this time, in this way, that I feel I must tender my resignation as College Physician for the Kent-Richmond College. I have found myself confronting personal issues lately that have forced a re-evaluation of the directions my life has taken. I am grateful and considerably in your debt for the trust you and your administration have put in me since my arrival at KRC. While I will always remember the personal mentoring and support you have provided me these past years as I learned to be not only a better doctor but a better administrator and person, I have discovered that I cannot continue as a part of the Kent-Richmond family.

Please rest assured that all is in order in my department and that you will find no unaccounted for funds or scandal awaiting my departure. Please know that this resignation has nothing to do your own leadership or my relations with other administrators at the College. It is simply the result of my own realization that I have actively sought for the past fifteen or so years, a life that is, by my own doing, incomplete.

My resignation is effective immediately. I seek no compensation for accrued vacation or sick time. I have arranged for my personal belongings to be picked up from the College's 'Bay House' by the end of the week.

My plans are vague. I seek to confront that within me which is lacking and the absence of which has kept me from true happiness. I may be reached through my mother's address in New York which is I believe, on file in the Personnel Office.

I am sorry for the inconvenience and trouble this sudden departure will cause you. Dr. Silva's office in the village will, I'm sure, be happy to help out during the transition. Please know that I have considered this course long and carefully before choosing it and that if there were a more professional way to handle this, I would choose it. I can only hope that the understanding you have

*shown with me before will once again enable you to accept what
I feel I must do.*

  Thanks once again, for everything.
  Sincerely,

  William Alexander Clark, MD

Alex set the machine to printing and padded into the kitchen to refill his coffee mug. When he returned to the computer the letter sat at the tray of his printer. It sat accusing him, in black and white, declaring his resolve, and affirming the desperate circumstances he had been struggling with.

He saved the letter to the hard drive and began another.

My Dearest Darcy,
  My only hope is that when you read this, and you hear about my departure from Kent, you will be able to understand that it is for the best.

  You of course know the increasing guilt I have felt about our relationship over the past few months. You of course know how bad I feel about us being together while your Eddie tries his best to be all that you deserve and need. I'm leaving Kent and "going to find myself".

  If that isn't a worn out, worthless expression, I don't know what is, but somehow it fits my worn out life.

  I'm sorry Babe. It has to be this way. You see, I appear to be in love with a memory. I've always been one kind of person and I've always been proud of who I was, but lately I've realized that I've been kidding myself. I've been safe and I've achieved. I've followed a good course. I've even done some good in the world but I've never really been complete. My goals and plans and tracks in life have always been a cop-out. I've always hidden behind the safety of my plans.

Afraid of Me

What I've finally realized is that what has been missing is the ability to face the things that intimidate me as they come, to be spontaneous. I've always planned my way around my fears and used my plans as an excuse for not taking the bold steps I knew, very deep down, that I had to take to be whole.

Look at us. I felt driven to begin our relationship but then felt it necessary to build it into a plan. It was a normal thing to do. There were sailing lessons and working together to blame it on. There were reasons. I've finally realized that the real reason for our relationship and for most of the things I've found myself mixed up in that weren't a part of my damn plans, were needs that I had denied. Our relationship didn't so much need to happen nor were there good reasons for it to happen, but it was a thing I needed to do to be a little more complete as a person.

I have lacked true courage in my life and the memories of an old friend have finally made me realize what has been missing all along.

You see Amy Hudson was a girl I knew in College. A friend I haven't even seen in at least ten years. Amy always challenged herself. Amy always faced the things she feared in life by doing them. I always dealt with the things I feared by hiding. The stability I've always been so proud of has been a sham. I've really been hiding. Just as I always thought Amy needed to be a lot more grounded in reality and safety, I now realize that I've always needed to be more able to face my fears.

I've always been in love with the idea of Amy but I could never understand why. Now that it's probably too late in my life to change, I understand. I don't even know if Amy is still alive or if she's been killed hang-gliding the Andes or staring down tigers in some Asian jungle. I just know that I've got to go find some of what she was to me.

Don't be jealous. It's not Amy herself I seek (I wouldn't begin to know where to look), it's what she represents to me—the other half of me.

Anyway, I've come to the conclusion that if I don't make a change in my life now, it will be too late for me forever. If I remain cloistered in my planned out, stable life, I'm sure to die a lonely, unfulfilled man. Maybe I'll go walk a beach somewhere. Maybe I'll end up in a gutter somewhere. All I know is that I've got to go.

I'll always remember and love you, kid. Give Eddie another chance if you can. I really think that is what's best for your life. I'm sorry to have led you astray and into my screwed up life.

Be well. Think of me once in a while.

Alex

Alex printed out this letter, repulsed at the ego it seemed to ooze but unable to say what he needed to more humbly. He felt events rushing toward him and knew that it was too late to stop and consider a safer course if he was ever to be able to make a change.

He put this letter into an envelope and addressed it to Darcy's on-campus office. He pulled up his earlier letter to his boss and faxed it directly to his office knowing that Dempsey wouldn't be in at least 'til noon on a Tuesday. Alex had spent enough time on the golf course with his boss to be pretty certain that was where he was today.

Alex put his coffee cup into the dishwasher, slipped his coat off the hook by the front door and with another glance in the mirror, shut the door to his Foreman's Cottage. By 9:30 he had emptied his savings and checking accounts at the Rhode Island Hospital Trust Bank on Warren Street, arranged to have his sailboat pulled out of the bay and stored until he called for it and was turning his black Saab south on I-95.

CHAPTER TWENTY-SIX

Four Winds and a Membership at the Waccabuc...

"Actually, Frank, the freedom is wonderful." Alex gazed at his companion across the slanting rays of sunshine splattering across the slate patio. "I don't profess to have it all figured out yet, but this is a pretty good life for now. The uncertainty of it all is actually quite refreshing. Poor old Mom doesn't quite understand. After all the years of hoping for stability and happiness for her children, for the eldest to suddenly chuck it all and move back in with her is a bit much."

"No, it's not really a problem for her to have me home. Since Dad passed away and my sister moved to Colorado, she's been kind of lonely anyway. As long as I keep telling her that I'm happier now than I've been in years, she's fine".

The man across the table smiled and shook his head. His black hair fell across his forehead just as it had in high school. The black framed glasses could have been the same ones he wore then too. Frank Niccosi had not changed significantly since he and Alex had played golf together as teenagers. Alex, it seemed, had.

"Well, my golf game is getting better," Alex continued. "I beat you today didn't I? I don't think I've done that since high school." He stretched, pleased with himself for the moment. He gazed across the eighteenth green and the fairway panorama spread out before them and thought back to a time when the clubhouse and golf course had seemed much more intimidating to them both.

"Remember how we used to sneak out here during the summer? The Pro used to be so pissed when he caught us— always threatening to have us arrested or, even worse, to call our parents. I swear if it wasn't for your girlfriend's Dad being a member, he really would have called the cops".

"Huh? Oh, I don't know about that", he responded to his old friend's questions. "It still feels a little funny being a member myself. Remember I've only been home four months now. I do love this course though. It reminds me of times before my life got so structured and forced. High school was great and even though we didn't have enough to join a Waccabuc Country Club then, life held enough challenges and joys".

"Remember the Fourth of July we snuck out here with those two girls? Yeah, we hardly knew them. I think we were as scared as they were. Boy, their fathers would not have been on our side. Life got so straight-laced and structured after those times".

"Bull. You did not know I'd become a boring person back then. That was well before my big plan." Responding now to Frank's teasing he rattled on, encouraged by a couple of cold beers after a hot afternoon on the course. "Hell, I thought you'd end up dealing drugs down in the Bronx with your cousins and look what a fat cat type you turned out to be," gesturing to Frank's rather increased girth.

"Well no you dork, beating you at golf doesn't add up to an exciting life for me now. I'm still looking for the courage to really challenge myself, to do some of the things I've always wanted to do. It's a partnership thing. I have to become a better partner for myself. I have to hold up my end with myself. I have to attend to all my needs—not just my needs for safety and security."

"I'm not really able yet to even articulate the things I want to do. I have to find a way to build up this new, risk-taker part of me. I have to learn to balance who I was with who I am and find the person I want to be. Its like I've only held up one side of a partnership with myself".

"Yeah, work helps. Remember Stephanie Banks who used to work at Four Winds. We all thought she was going to go crazy because she spent all her time trying to help the crazy people at that Loony Bin. I never really knew much about the place when I lived here. Some of the very best families have people in there. They can afford private care and Four Winds is very private".

"Yeah, they focus on alcohol and drug treatment these days," getting a little more serious for a moment. "Its pretty interesting stuff for someone like me who has been treating sore throats and stomach cramps all his professional life. And shift work is just fine for me for now. No way do I want to put down too many roots right away. You know, I even negotiated a delay on my initiation here at the Club in case I wasn't here more than a year".

"Hell no, I don't mind not working every day. Aren't you listening, my friend? Have another beer. The whole point of doing fill-in, on-call work is so that I can turn it down when a hot pigeon like you becomes available for a little thrashing on the golf course. And besides, treating the ailments of people wrestling with life-threatening addictions," looking now at his friend for some approval or understanding, "is much more challenging and interesting than treating menstrual cramps in little girls with nothing more important to wrestle with than sophomore chemistry".

"What? Oh yeah, the sophomores were most often cuter than the alcoholics but the nurses here are just as cute".

125

CHAPTER TWENTY-SEVEN

Home At Least...

Amy Hudson strolled down the main street of Clifton Falls. She walked head down mostly, not in any hurry to get anywhere, no real purpose in her step. She wandered. She looked around herself occasionally, at the once familiar homes and streets. She saw the tree-lined neighborhoods but didn't really register them as her own. Her shambling pace and casual jeans and striped top seemed to emphasize the lost feeling she still had. The cool breeze blowing her long brown hair, hanging straight to her shoulders, brushed the hair across her face occasionally but she did not bother to brush it back behind her ears.

In the lulls between cars on a warm summer evening like this, she could hear the rumble of trucks on the interstate rolling across the fields. At night she could see the bright lights of Albany reflected in the sky above. She reached the end of Main Street proper, where it forked to the left and to the right. The road forked down to the left under the railroad tracks and up to the right to parallel them into Albany. She knew that under the tracks the road quickly found farmland and corn to wander through. She knew also that to the right it ran into Route 9W and became more and more congested and urban the closer it got to the state capital. She was close enough to that busy little city to feel it yet out here, she remained surrounded by the slow, quiet pace of the countryside.

Amy paused at the fork and thought about the different worlds the different directions could take a person—did take a person. Growing up in Clifton Falls, she had hated the open fields in winter and the tall corn in summer. She had yearned for what she thought awaited her up the road in Albany. It had symbolized, for her, the gateway to a bigger, more exciting world and it had, in fact, been all of that.

Her parent's home a few blocks away was in someone else's hands now. The storefronts she had just passed had different looks and different tenants. The Presbyterian Church was now the Library. The Candy Store now rented videos. It looked different and was, she guessed, some else's hometown now. Still, it helped her to think more than she had anticipated it would.

After her medical discharge, she had realized she really had no where to go back to. After being paid off and kissed off by the Army, she had wandered back to Clifton Falls. The just past week in the Motel at the truck stop near the highway was not exactly what she had been looking for, but at least she was beginning to be able to think again.

It had been a long time since she had allowed herself to think much. It was shock related the medics said. Prolonged traumatic reaction syndrome, they called it. Seeing Dwayne run down, holding his crushed, beautiful head in her arms, hearing the life gurgle out of him had been too much to accept. It had happened too suddenly.

She shuddered even though it was a warm night. She looked up and to the right, shuddered again, and continued walking, down and to the left, under the bridge and out to the quiet, simple fields.

Dwayne's death had been the precipice over which she had fallen. It had been a long, terrible downward spiral. She was sure she knew how passengers trapped in a crashing, falling airliner must feel, knowing that the bottom is coming up fast and having no way to control the descent.

Her initial month of hardship leave had been extended to two. Even though the Army had initially fought their inter-racial, officer/enlisted person, same department, overseas marriage, they had done their best to be accommodating after Dwayne's death.

If he had died in the line of duty it might have been easier for her to understand, she thought for the thousandth time. If it hadn't been so pointless it might have been better in some perverse way.

Dwayne was just too good. He had insisted on stopping to help the old couple with the flat. He had insisted that it was no trouble to change their tire for them in spite of the driving rain. Amy had insisted that she too could be of help, even if it was only to hold the umbrella in his general direction.

The truck had seemed huge. It had come out of the rain just a little too fast. It was just a little too dark and raining just a little too hard. Dwayne, damn him, was just a little too far out in the road. It was really nobody's fault.

Without him, the spiral had been steep, the fall far and fast. Amy had ended up "under observation"—suicide watch actually. She had been hospitalized for a time and then sent, smiling weakly, back to duty. She had made plans to transfer back to the states, a fresh start and all that. But when it came time to leave for Florida, she couldn't be moved. It wasn't that she refused as much as she couldn't. She couldn't get on that plane. She couldn't leave the base or the barracks apartment she had moved into after leaving the hospital. She couldn't risk.

The transfer was canceled. Her duty assignments reduced. She was basically reduced to clerk work. She went back into counseling. It had been a long haul.

A year had passed since Dwayne's death when the Army finally made the decision to muster her out. She could check herself into any VA hospital she wanted, whenever she felt she needed it. She had requested mustering out to the Albany area. The good VA hospital there made the Army feel better. It was there for a lack of a better idea as far as she was concerned.

CHAPTER TWENTY-EIGHT

Roots Are For Trees...

Amy awoke in the Traveler's Rest Motel and Truck Stop just off I-87 on Route 9W. She had been in residence at room 115 for three weeks now. The eighteen-wheelers rumbled in and out day and night but she took little notice. The big rigs were something she once knew but took little interest in now. Their lower, more streamlined noses seemed somewhat perverse to her. Their attempts to look modern and save a little gas in the bargain only seemed to make more obvious how long it had been since she had ridden her own big, square, Cabover Peterbilt.

Long walks through old haunts hadn't helped her find her path. None of the old places had been able to suggest a new direction. She felt insulated from herself. She was afraid in a way she hadn't felt in a long, long time. She felt as though if she reached, if she risked, it would all come tumbling down again. Something inside her screamed out in confirmation of what her mother had said all those years ago—that all that risk was just thrill seeking and thrill seeking could only end up in heartbreak.

Had Momma been right? Had all her fear facing led her, inevitably, to heartache and this immobilization of her soul?

Amy knew that she couldn't stay at the Traveler's Rest forever but she couldn't, for the life of her, decide what to do or where to go next. There were no challenges to confront that didn't terrify her. There was nothing that she felt she could conquer without Dwayne. All her old adventures seemed trite and meaningless. Trips and jobs and relationships that had seemed to be helping her to grow were now just painful reminders of a seemingly wasted youth. It felt like a hole had been burned into her soul and all the desires and needs and fears had leaked out. Now all that was left was an ache where the hole was, memories where her heart had once been and the fear that she would never again be alive.

Her disability pension from the service had kept her Motel bill paid so far. She didn't, in fact, seem to be able to spend what she was allowed. Dwayne's savings were hers as well, although they still sat untouched in a New York City bank. Nothing seemed important enough in Amy's life to invest his legacy in.

There was nothing to do, no place for her to go. Nothing caught her eye or piqued her interest. She sat, she walked, she thought. Her solitary existence formed a cocoon about her, insulating her from the world and all its hurts. She withdrew into the cocoon and felt nothing. Nothing was safe.

On the Thursday of Amy's third week at the Traveler's, she encountered Bobbie. Bobbie was a small girl, certainly not a woman yet. Her long, stringy hair was a little stiff and needed a good combing out. Bobbie had shaved one side of her head, from the looks of it by herself, had apparently not showered in several days and seemed destined to live forever in the cut-off jeans, pierced belly button-exposing short top and orange Keds.

Amy found Bobbie sitting at the side door to the Traveler's upon returning from her morning walk to Clifton Falls and back. Sitting alone at the side door to a truck-stop motel, looking tired and a little dirty, obviously waiting for something, she brought Amy up short.

Amy approached the hungry looking waif as if confronting a ghost. She asked her name and if she could help her. Bobbie, with an afraid yet defiant little voice, explained that she was waiting for a trucker she had been traveling with to get back from a pick-up at his depot and that she was sure that he'd be back to pick her up soon.

How long had she been waiting, Amy asked.

"Since early the previous evening," was the answer.

"What company does he work for," Amy asked?

"Overnight Express."

"What was his name?"

"Jim something."

"What was his cab number?" Bobbie wasn't sure.

"Where was she headed?" Bobbie wasn't sure.

"Could you use a hot shower," Amy asked?

"Sure I could, but I can't miss Jim when he gets back," Bobbie replied with no hint of suspicion.

Amy arranged to watch for Jim while Bobbie had used her room to shower and clean up. When she checked on her after forty-five minutes, she found the thin, child-like thing asleep on her bed in 115. Amy waited and they talked when Bobbie awoke.

They decided together that Jim probably wasn't coming back. Over dinner they decided that perhaps Rochester wasn't the end of the world despite what Bobbie had decided before hitching out two days earlier. They decided that Bobbie should have a plan before leaving Rochester again forever.

Amy found herself encouraging Bobbie to create a safety net for herself. She shared her own experiences on the road and pointed out some of the things she had learned to be wary of. Bobbie was a good listener and allowed that perhaps she shouldn't have waited so late into the summer to begin her escape. She allowed too that there was a family back in Rochester waiting for her, that they were, in fact, probably worried sick.

Finally she allowed that even if Kurt Fitzpatrick had dumped her for another girl, there were probably better ways to get back at him. Perhaps, she admitted, making something of her self was a better payback.

As a plan began to come together in her head—College in the fall on the art scholarship she had been offered, seeing the world as a traveling artist rather than a helpless waif, leaving Kurt and his Kodak plant fork lift behind rather than running without a destination—Bobbie began to re-energize. She regained some of the animation that Amy was sure was behind her sad, brown eyes.

By Noon Friday, Bobbie was on a bus pulling out of the downtown Albany station headed west toward Rochester.

By 4:00 p.m. the next day, Amy was packing up her used VW convertible. She checked out of the Traveler's, the owner of a new plan herself. She trembled considerably at the uncertainty of a new adventure and a new beginning. Nonetheless, she took the first steps toward rather than away.

As she turned in her key, she noticed a mailbox just inside the lobby door. She rummaged around inside her shoulder bag and pulled out a slightly wrinkled postcard of the New York State Capital building. The Postcard, addressed to one Dr. William Alexander Clark, told in tiny but expressive print, of new hopes, of wanting to see him to talk of old times, of having finally figured out something of what he had been trying to tell her on a porch, fifteen years earlier. It suggested that she would contact him when she got settled and that she would tell him then about her new plans.

Laugh lines crinkled around the brown eyes and creases formed around the expressive mouth as it smiled a warm remembrance. Freckles once again brought out by the long summer walks stood out on cheeks surrounding a slightly pug nose. Rummaging further until she found the tiny address book in the bottom of the bag she addressed the card, in care of Kent-Richmond College in Rhode Island, dropped it in the slot and walked slowly out into the sunshine.

CHAPTER TWENTY-NINE

Searching...

Baxter hadn't changed that much, Alex decided. It was still obviously a College town. So much of the town depended on the students that even with the change in the drinking age, Main Street was still lined with bars that catered to the annual invasion. His old haunts had become a little more subtle now, but most were still there.

Alex decided that the absence of giant signs in the windows advertising weekend and weekday drink and beer specials gave Main Street less character. He decided that cleaner and more controlled was not necessarily better when it came to college town character.

Alex parked the Saab in the municipal lot. He rolled up the windows and locked it but did not bother to hide the suitcase and golf bag thrown across the back seat as he might have felt compelled to in other days. He buttoned the thin jacket he wore and turned up the collar against the early autumn breeze. Not much more golf this season he thought.

The change in the weather had instigated his decision to move on again from Westchester and Four Winds and the Waccabuc. They play golf all year 'round down south he had thought. They have hospitals down there too. Heck, Baxter was just an hour or so out of his way, why not take a look? Maybe his old stomping grounds would help him find some of the answers he was looking for.

After a ride through the campus and a walk through the new Rec. Center building, his team's trophies dusty in a new display case along one wall, he drove downtown, intending to look around and then catch a little lunch before heading on. He planned to try to make the D. C. area by nightfall.

He walked down Main to Oak and turned down hill to where The Friendly Lion had been. He had a beer in the same room he had frequented as an eighteen year-old although it was now called Ernie's Attic. Funny he thought, it hadn't moved upscale at all, the bar was still in the same place, it still smelled vaguely like the stale air than escapes from a dead keg, but it had given itself a new name and the kids in it had created their own new memories for the room.

He left the Lion/Attic and turned at the corner to Mill Street. He walked past General Clinton's Pub and the spot where the Cadillac Disco had been. He turned again on Chestnut and slowly walked past the Brooks Department Store and back to Main. At the corner of Main and Chestnut he paused.

Where was it? It should be two, no three doors down the block. There, next to the Ski and Sport Shop, that's where The Novelty should be. It was gone though. The Novelty Lounge had finally passed into the oblivion of the memories of those who had frequented it. Surprised, Alex realized that he had half expected it to still be there, with Gracey at the bar ready to give him a disapproving look for being absent for so many years. In its place, occupying the same space, he now found—a bookstore of all things.

Alex drifted toward the bookstore. Perhaps it would somehow still resemble the Novelty inside as Ernie's Attic had resembled The Lion. Perhaps books would be arranged on the old stage and the cashier would be standing behind Gracey's bar.

CHAPTER THIRTY

Return of the Bookworm...

Three months out of counseling, the closest VA hospital is in
Syracuse. My job is steady and low stress. My little apartment is
quiet. I guess I've reverted back to the bookworm I was before
ever coming here. I find my solace in books now just as I found my
adventures in books back in my high school days. Today I read
and live with my books, immerse myself in their stories, find
comfort in their warm friendship. I can live from day to day now.
The haunting fears and thoughts of Germany are fading, kept at
bay by the normalcy of my existence here in Baxter.

Nobody remembers me here and I think that's good. Most of
my old professors are retired or gone, not that I paid them much
attention fifteen years ago.

Dixon and Michaels and company have given way to a new
bunch of trash and they express no interest in the new resident of
Center Street. The Novelty is gone and Gracey is in Florida
somewhere. It's the same old town with a new batch of faces,
familiar yet different, safe yet engaging enough to keep my mind
busy.

The new students are a lot like we were twenty years ago,
fresh, inquisitive, testing their limits. Those I get to know seem
nice enough, and if we get to talking long enough and I get a peek

at their goals and aspirations, they at least humor me by seeming to care about the advice I try to give them. I guess I know its advice they won't really listen to. They have to find their own ways and face their own dragons but it makes me feel good to give it.

All that's missing is someone like Alex. I miss that tall, lean, young/old face, that friend and guardian, that listener and judge. I think part of what I still need is someone like him. Nobody here has interested me that way. Even though I now realize there will eventually be someone after Dwayne, I guess I'm just not ready yet. Alex's probably happily married again by now—he wouldn't have it any other way, I'm sure. He's probably working on his two point third child. I guess I'm not surprised that he hasn't responded to my postcards.

Old Doctor Alex is probably driving a station wagon and wearing sensible shoes to the office. I really feel love for that stodgy old friend. I really feel like I finally understand what he tried to say by all those judging frowns and worried words so long ago. I think he was trying to tell me that it was OK to be a little afraid, OK to hang back a little, OK to risk less than it all.

I could sure use one of his big bear hugs these days…it's funny how we remember things. In my mind I still see him as a thin young man, a little too tall and a little too awkward when he had something to say. I wonder what he looks like these days. There, that man in the front of the store, tall and bearded, sort of tweedy around the edges, salt and pepper in his beard and temples, I'll bet that's what he looks like today. I bet he's still as handsome as I once thought he was.

This guy could use a hair cut. He doesn't look like he's really interested in buying a book. He looks more like a tourist, on his way somewhere and just stopping in for something to do.

Gee, he looks about the same height as I remember Alex to be. I wonder if Alex has gotten fat or whether he's taken care of himself like this guy has.

Well, better see if this guy wants some help.

CHAPTER THIRTY-ONE

This Time She Wasn't Screaming...

Alex entered The Leading Edge bookstore and looked around. A Fleetwood Mac tune from' 73 or '74 murmured softly from the overhead speakers. Gracey's bar was completely gone. A false wall had been put up across the back of the room concealing some kind of storeroom. The room was bright too. The front window had been enlarged and rows of fluorescents ran down the center of the still-high ceiling. No bar, no stage, no pool table; it was hard to picture what had been. A counter and computer sat near the front, almost where Gracey's register had been he guessed. Rows of wooden bookshelves stuck out from the left-hand wall where the booths had been. More shelves lined the opposite wall, where the bar and stage had been. The effect was disorienting. It was the same space but different. Unlike The Lion, this room seemed to have shed its memories with a shudder. Not content to merely let new memories in the front door, it seemed to have thrown the old memories out the back.

Alex wandered around the front of the store; not really interested in the books and magazines he picked up and discarded. He just didn't want to look like he was staring. Oh well, he thought, another memory overtaken by time.

Now he looked more carefully at the magazine in his hand— *Modern Boating*. A woman was approaching from the back of the store and he figured he should at least know what he held if asked. He supposed he should buy something.

He looked up as the woman approached. She was of medium height; healthy looking, if a bit thin, her short, dark hair was pulled back behind one ear and secured with a barrette. A smallish nose held up metal-framed glasses, which in turn framed rather pretty brown eyes. She was pretty average at first glance, a little pale and drawn, as if she hadn't had a good night's sleep. Alex looked down at his magazine, feigning interest until she asked if he needed any help. He looked up then, looked at the mouth that had produced a vaguely familiar voice. Her mouth was expressive, full-lipped and a little broad. She smiled readily at his startled look, a quizzical squint coming into her eyes.

"Amy?" he said a little breathlessly, feeling immediately stupid for giving voice to the possibility. She looked right through him, her thoughts elsewhere. The room began to close in just a little, an echo of long ago disco music ringing against his ears from a jukebox long removed from the room.

"Yes?" she replied, still smiling but with no hint of recognition. "Can I help you?"

Alex looked again. The hair was a little darker than he remembered. Her height was about right but there was a leanness his memory did not register. Although her figure was still slender and curved in the right places her simple, V-neck top and loose fitting Dockers didn't invite particular attention to it. She was thin at the waist and along the jaw line, almost too thin.

Alex felt his face flush.

The picture in his memory flickered in conflict with the image of the woman in front of him. There were lines around the eyes and mouth but the mouth fit the memory. The nose, although still small, now had a slight twist to the left, obviously broken somewhere along the line. He stared at her for what seemed like a long time. She shifted nervously and began to edge slightly into a more easily defensible position. In her eyes he saw a little fear, a little measuring of him and, finally a quizzical, questioning need to understand the tall, scruffy, bearded stranger in her store.

"Amy?" He asked again. Then, pointing a thumb at his own chest, he ventured, "Alex."

She looked at him for what seemed another long, silent moment—evaluation, memory and then recognition flashing across her eyes. Disbelief came next and then acceptance and she had her arms around his neck. She almost knocked him into the magazine rack. She didn't say a word, hung on for all her might, tears suddenly in her warm, lonely, lovely eyes.

"You got my letters." she finally whispered into his ear—not a question but a statement. "You came to rescue me again," as if she had expected his arrival any time.

SIX

TODAY

CHAPTER THIRTY-TWO

... No Longer Afraid

"Cave diving! Haven't you ever seen on those National Geographic Specials, how cool it is to be in an underwater cave?" Amy bubbled with enthusiasm as she rifled through the assembled booklets and brochures scattered across the thick throw rug. "It's so beautiful down there! I've always wanted to learn to dive and to do it really right we could go to a place where you can cave dive!" Her enthusiasm was genuine.

"Amy my love, you're doing it again," Alex replied with mock seriousness. "Let's start with open water diving first. Maybe a little reef snorkeling, then some scuba classes in a nice, safe pool. There'll be plenty of time to decide that we can't live without closing ourselves off from the entire outside world in a cave."

"Oh come on Alex, let go a little, you don't have to always play by the rules. This place says they have you dive certified in two days and then they take you right to the caves."

"OK, OK, but it doesn't have to be all adventure does it? Can't we pick an island with a couple of golf courses too?"

"Don't 'OK' me Dr. Clark. I can tell when you're just humoring me." Amy smiled and wrapped her arms around Alex's neck. She drew his face down to hers and kissed it. She held him close and looked lovingly into his eyes. Her own eyes got that long ago dreamt of quizzical look in them and her brow furrowed ever so slightly. She kissed him again briefly and smiled.

"What kind of honeymoon do you prescribe old Dr. Clark?"

Alex looked into Amy's warm, smiling, happy eyes. The haunted look was gone. The hurt just below the surface was no longer so evident. She felt good against him. Firm yet soft, warm and relaxed.

There was such a difference from when he had first found her again. He'd like to take the credit for the turn around, he told himself, but he knew that he shouldn't. Amy had healed herself. She had put away her demons and fears. She had come back to herself. Amy had taken herself past what had made her afraid. Sure his being there, falling all over himself with love and gratitude for this second chance had probably helped. Perhaps their time together had let her know that she was once again worth loving. Perhaps his being there had given her permission to be a whole person again. Perhaps she just needed to be valued again.

He pulled her closer, put one big hand on each side of her slender waist, almost encircling her. He slid his hand up to feel her gentle curves, her strong shoulders. He lovingly encircled her neck with his forearms and ran his fingers through her lengthening wavy brown and blond streaked hair.

She had certainly shaped up since their chance meeting in Baxter he thought again. She had, though, done it herself. Once on the road to wholeness again she had attacked it like she had attacked all her old challenges, pulling strength and energy from the work around her once again.

This time, Alex had hung on for the ride and relished the bumps. He had been determined, almost from the moment he had first seen her, not to let her go again.

Two individuals searching the world for the part of them that was missing they had, in finding each other again, almost immediately seen that what they had lacked all along was each other.

Why had it taken two semi-intelligent people almost twenty years to see that what they had each lacked was each other? They had debated that question long into the night on a number of occasions. There didn't seem to be any rush to find out that answer now though. Since that late summer day in Baxter, they had been inseparable. Long walks, intimate fireside evenings, long autumn bicycle rides exploring the countryside as they had long years ago had made them comfortable with each other once again.

They talked and talked. They discovered that they both needed to get it all out to each other. At first Alex couldn't stop talking about Julie and the pain her leaving had caused him.

"She left me empty. I hid from myself. I felt insulated and alone even around people."

As he talked he realized how much he had wanted to share this pain with someone and for how long.

It helped Alex to talk, as he had heretofore not talked to another soul about the self-doubts Julie's departure had left within him. He talked because he knew that Amy could understand and would not judge. Alex talked about the years of surviving on surface successes without a soul of his own underneath it all. He talked about realizing that he had settled in life, settled for less than he could have had and less than he had even allowed himself to dream.

Amy shared the pain that had driven her within herself, the only pain she had ever been unable to face—when Dwayne had been taken from her. Amy talked about the dreams she had passed up on the road to herself. She realized finally that she had been so wrapped up in seeking the next big challenge, that she could seldom savor an individual moment. She had never made love, she told Alex, until they were finally together. She had never been able to let go and just be with a man. Always analyzing and comparing and watching from the outside, she had denied herself the opportunity to be inside during her own experiences.

They talked of all that he could have been save for the courage to let go and live and of all that she could have had but for the courage to deal with herself rather than the external stimuli of a world that, in the end, didn't care.

Finally they had decided, given a second chance that neither had ever expected, that what they had lacked all along was each other. Amy could relax now with Alex, knowing that she would be loved and accepted with nothing to prove. Alex could let go of his charted course and live, knowing that he would not be judged and that he too would have nothing to prove.

Alex and Amy could love and be loved. They could make love to each other, finally secure in the knowledge that they had found balance. His months of wandering and years of settling could come to an end knowing that Amy would always spur him to be more than he would otherwise be. She could attack life with somewhat less abandon than she always had, no longer fearing what any less would leave her with.

It was astonishing to both how quickly they came to the same conclusion. They each made the other whole and together they were what the other had always needed. To expect that they would ever again accept any less than each other seemed absurd.

Within two weeks they had hit the road with no particular agenda. The apartment was sublet and the Saab was sold in deference to the VW's ragtop. The ties with Baxter once again were cut.

They traveled in the little convertible through a cleansing New England fall, flush with colors. They got to know each other again riding the wave of colors through Vermont and New Hampshire. In Maine they found a Bed and Breakfast by the rocky shore and learned love as they had never learned it before. They touched and explored and nervous as teenagers, received pleasure in the giving as much as in the taking. His hands felt her curves and felt her smoothness. Her hands played with his chest hair and pulled his bearded face down to her. Back down the coast to Cape Cod, they walked the quiet streets of off-season Provincetown and the windy stretches of white sand. Hand in hand they collected tiny shells at Race Point Beach.

They stopped in Kent and Alex had seemed so happy and whole that all but the most bitter of his former colleagues decided that his departure had been for the best. They checked that Alex's sailboat had been properly stored and the way he beamed while showing her through it made Amy warm inside despite the cold and windy weather.

Christmas had been time with Alex's Mom and both Alex and Amy found themselves filled with the spirit of the season for the first time in years. New Year's Eve brought an immersion in the Times Square crowd and a new ability to let go of the past. Healthy and happy once again they had welcomed springtime together on a windswept Carolina beach. Running the beach at dawn and walking the tide each evening, Amy and Alex found themselves, together.

After a while, Alex felt that he could return to work. He felt, finally, that he *should* return to work. Not this time though to a safe, uncomplicated practice where the complaints didn't tax his skills but to a place where he felt he would be needed.

Amy soon found an article in a drug store magazine. She wrote to the organization that had been the topic of the article. By the time Alex found out, the interview had been arranged. They drove up to Philadelphia in the VW and in two months he had his assignment. Alex and Amy would move together once more. A small village in Lee County, Virginia would become their first home together.

The rural farmland that looked out over the Shenandoah Valley and up the slopes of the Blue Ridge Mountains was largely unchanged since Civil War armies had ranged up and down the valley below. Alex would be a small town doctor in these hills. He would be their only doctor; in fact the only doctor in Lee County. He would handle all the medical challenges thrown at the residents of these hills by life in these hills. He would not be able to refer patients to colleagues down the road if things got busy or difficult. He would have to handle those who could not afford the trip to Roanoke to the hospital as well as those who could not survive that trip. He would have to work without a net.

As soon as they saw this new country they would share, Amy decided to go to work too. While Alex set up shop in downtown Spring Hill, Amy had driven the back roads in their new Jeep for hours on end. Each night she brought a head full of ideas and possibilities home to an exhausted Alex.

Finally she had decided, and the purchase of a few acres had been arranged and she had gone to work. Their cabin home was now almost finished. The trails to the lake and the trout stream had been cut and subtly marked, the trees had been trimmed just enough to ensure a year round view of the valley below. Built entirely by her own hand, Amy's cabin was a marvel to Alex. Not a nail showed in the planking either inside or out. The fireplace hearth and chimney stood firmly of native stone. The great room was furnished with tables and chairs fashioned from the birch and pine cleared to make room for the house. The Jeep was nestled in its own little lean to on one side.

"I prescribe a honeymoon where there are both caves to dive in and golf courses to play on. I prescribe a honeymoon where there are no hammers or saws, no old farmers with worn out feet or young children in need of a dentist. I prescribe a honeymoon with you Mrs. Clark, with you and you alone."

THE END